Somewhere south

A novel

Will Levington Comfort

Alpha Editions

This edition published in 2023

ISBN : 9789357969918

Design and Setting By
Alpha Editions
www.alphaedis.com
Email - info@alphaedis.com

Contents

PROLOGUE

OLD LIGHTS OF THE RIO BRAVA

I

BOB LEADLEY moved toward the sound of guitars. The strumming came from over the stream where the Mexicans had their own little cantina and their dobe huts. Back from the 'Damask Cheek,' which was the palpitating core of the white settlement, voices of the miners reached him, not loud to-night, not uproarious. Things were seldom duller than now on the Rio Brava, shrunken to a trickle at this time of year. The eke of gold had been at its lowest for days on the placers. A hot, still August night in Bismo, Arizona—the night that changed one white man all around.

Mexican figures bowed to him. A woman laughingly called from a darkened doorway: 'Buenas noches, señor!' Another laughed from behind her, adding somewhat wistfully: 'Hace un calor sofocante.'

He walked on past the dobe huts and on to the mesa. He heard the coyotes—different from any time before. There was no moon and the stars were indistinct, run together in the heat haze. Bob Leadley took off his hat; drops of sweat held by the tight hatband, dropped down on his face. He had to laugh at himself—the feelings that rolled and tumbled over each other within. Nobody would have believed it of him—feelings to keep a secret of. It was as if some one he had always been waiting for, had come to town—not yet seen, a friend or enemy, he couldn't tell, but a life-or-death meaning to the arrival. Running steps reached him from behind; a panting voice calling:

'Bob! Bob!'

'Hello, Mort,' he answered as the other came up, the tone so quiet and cool, it was almost whimsical.

'What you doing away off here?'

'She didn't want me there.'

'It's a boy, Bob, only—'

'I thought as much.'

'It's a boy all right, only she—they say she ain't going to live.'

The mother was already dead, but this was Mort Cotton's way of softening the shock for a friend.

The same easy tone answered: 'Guess we'd better walk back.'

'I wouldn't hurry, if I was you. Bob. I'll run back if you like and get the rest of the word.'

It was her doings that they called the child Bart, after some saint of her religion. She had a lot of saints, one for every day or so—a Spanish woman, and she hadn't asked much, come to think of it.

The oddest thing Bob Leadley had ever done was to marry her. He never would have thought better of it, except it made a difference in the town. It would make more of a difference now—leaving a boy with her blood in his veins. They wouldn't call it 'Spanish' blood in Bismo. Mexicans weren't held high on this side of the Border.... Queer little birdlike ways, she had—little vanities and secrets—always shrinking farther indoors in daylight, always more alive in the night time. She had sung and cooked and washed for him; pleasant to be with, but he never really knew her. She was like ripe fruit that couldn't last—pleasant to the taste and pretty to look at, but nothing much for real hunger. Come and gone with her curious ways, her brightenings up in the dark—only asking one thing—that the boy be called after this particular one of her saints, and 'Bart' was as good a name as any.

So there was a gray-eyed white man in Bismo, Arizona, with a black-eyed boy in his cabin. No problem about it at all, from the standpoint of the other miners, just scorn—only Bob Leadley had been known from away back as cool and gamy as they made them; nothing like the squaw-man, cholo-man type. The miners couldn't give much play to their contempt before those pleasant gray eyes of Bob's, which might inquire their meaning, and look into it. Men weren't mind-readers in Bismo. They saw the steady eyes, the whimsical smile, but no one knew what was going on; not even Mort Cotton, who had punched cattle, skinned mules, and washed for gold with Bob Leadley for ten years; not even the Mexican woman and her daughter who brought Bart up. But it was all a matter of how you gave advice. Bismo found out gradually that Bob wasn't set up very high in his idea of being a successful parent. They found he listened attentively to comment given within a certain range of tones; discovering this, the miners supplied it plentifully.

The social barrier in Bismo was the river itself. Mexican laborers worked, two to one to the white men, in the placers, but the two settlements rarely mixed outside working hours, except when waves of drink inundated the white miners. Then they would move over to Dobe-town to drink and 'eat different,' the calls ending in a row, not infrequently in the death of a 'greaser.' Letchie Welton, the town marshal, wasn't even to be approached on a matter like this, and sounds of mourning from one or more dobe huts seldom reached as far as the 'Damask Cheek,' any more than the strumming of guitars....

Several times in the next dozen years, Bob Leadley and Mort Cotton were on the point of leaving Bismo, but the Rio Brava had a way of suddenly picking up, the gold eke rising to quite a little color. There was another thing; it was hard for Bob to make up his mind to take Bart away from the Mexican woman and her daughter. It didn't seem fair. The old señora had been a friend of Bart's mother and loved the white man's boy; also her daughter loved him. But Bart was growing up more Mexican than white; talked Spanish in preference to English; was more often seen across the stream than on this side, and running with the Mexican boys, one Palto especially, than with the four or five white boys of his age in town. Bart's whole business was horses, but Mexican words having to do with them were too easy on his tongue—hondos, latigos, reatas, conchos, yakimas. A slim, black-haired youth, slow to rouse, not cruel or a fool; an easy way with him; not stirred in the least by the thought of washing gold; no idea of working hours, as being superior to all others.

Just to see Bart leaning against the doorway—on his feet, but relaxed in a way no white boy could stand, a guitar in his hand, perhaps—had a way of filling his father with a revulsion that Bob had to take out to the mesa to quiet. It was as if the man saw the face of his boy under a high-tinted sombrero (instead of the cast-off cavalryman's campaign hat with a Copley peak) as if a sash of seda were thrust back over the shoulder. Bob didn't quite know it, but it was because he was seeing Bart with the eyes of the other miners at these times—that he was stung so. The town had put a secret fear on him that his boy was not showing up white.

The father lacked one thing that parents usually have to work with. He didn't have the sense of being right at all times. Once or twice he felt so sure of himself that he treated Bart to a whipping, which the boy took without a murmur, minding pain no more than an Indian. He never explained. The father got one of the starts of his life to find he had whipped Bart for a thing he didn't do, the boy not taking the trouble to clear himself. Bob's feeble sense of rightness was shaken by that; it about all went out of him, and something else with it. The deep hurt of it was that Bart held no grievance afterward.

A master at letting other men alone, Bob couldn't keep his thoughts and his will-power off the boy. He made up for his rare rough periods by being lenient. All the time his actions and reactions brought advice from his fellow townsmen. It was Letchie Welton, the town marshal, who started the saying that Bart wouldn't live to be hanged. All this time Bob Leadley's eyes were the most light-hearted anywhere.

'As a male-parent, I'm considerable of a botch—I admit that,' he would say, in a way to delude anybody that he ever suffered real care, and at the same time there was a sorrow burning at the center of him like a red lamp. Often at work on the placer, he knew a loneliness to get close to his boy. He might have seen Bart at breakfast, but that made no difference. He felt lonely for him more than once, when they were in the same room together.

II

BART was past twelve, when he was missing for a day or two, and rode back into town on a gray rat-tailed pony that was raked from shoulder to crupper with fresh wounds and old scars. Letchie Welton, in the capacity of deputy sheriff, halted him at the edge of town, looking the outfit over.

'Where did you get that briscut?'

'Over at the Cup Q.'

'Did you do all that fresh hookin' on his hide?'

'No.'

'Buy him?'

'No, they didn't want him much over at the rancho. Said I could have him for sitting thirty seconds—'

'And you did?'

'Yep—more. I ain't got off.'

Letchie Welton looked queer and rode back to the placers where he found Bob Leadley. 'Your kid's just brought in a man-killer from the Cup Q—a gray rat-tail I remember seein' over there. If I was you, Bob, I'd put a bullet in the head of that cayuse, and I'd leave off work and do it now—before he kicks a hole out of Bart's face or eats his scalp off.' Letchie Welton went on to recall further details of Rat-tail's reputation—of the fits he threw, the men he had maimed.

Bob left the placer and went to his own little corral where he found Rat-tail unsaddled, Bart leaning in the fence shadow, looking over his new possession.

'I hear he's an outlaw, Bart. I wouldn't ride him if I was you.'

'I rode him over from the Cup Q all right.'

'I know. He may have been glad to get away from there—but look at him!' Bob took a few steps closer to the old gray head which suddenly looked deformed. A float of baleful red appeared back of the near, filmy eye.

'I've seen that look once or twice before, Bart, and I'll have to tell you to stay off him.'

'All he knew from the Cup Q was rakin' and quirtin', Dad.'

'But that ain't the look of a nice hoss.'

'I like him.'

'It ain't the look of a broke hoss, Bart.'

'I don't want no broke hoss.'

'You'll have to stay off, that's all—'

Bob saw that deep questioning look in the eyes slowly turned his way—no anger, no hate, but separateness, a widening gulf.

'At least, stay off him till I try him out for a few days.'

Bob was sincere in his attempt to make the rat-tail safe for his son, but the toughest saddle-sessions he had ever known, followed in the next ten days. Where the ordinary outlaw left off with sun-fish and rail-fence, the old gray opened fresh spontaneities. One of the last things he did with Bob forked, was to make a quarter-mile sprint toward a low-hanging cottonwood limb, the idea being to rake off his tormentor, which he carried out. Another time when Bob persisted several seconds longer than usual, the rat-tail came out of a buckling snap—to fling himself on the ground. The day came when Bob Leadley, cool-eyed, a smile on his lips, would have preferred to stand up and be shot at, than mount the gray monster again, but that's what he did, it being his code. That day Rat-tail plunged into a dobe wall and left Bart's father on the inside of a crowded chicken yard with a broken leg.

'I should have done what Letchie told me, Bart,' Bob said that night. 'He ain't a man-killer just; he's a man-eater. You'll have to leave him alone from now on.'

'You tried hookin' him, the way they did over in the Cup Q. It makes him crazy. He ain't crazy natural, his mouth's tender. He's been driven crazy. He needs humorin', Dad.'

Anger flamed up in the father. He had been a horse-hand all his life. 'I say keep off him, from now on.'

Three days later Mort Cotton came into the cabin, his bushy eyebrows showing curiously white. 'I hate to tell on the kid, Bob, but it'll get to you anyway,' he said. 'He's been riding that rat-tail on a hackamore—he's ridin' him now. And what I'm gettin' at is, he ain't havin' trouble.'

Bob's face turned to the wall. He had many days to think it out while his leg was in boards.... It was disobedience, but had he been right? Didn't Bart have something on the gray others hadn't—with other horses, too, perhaps? It wasn't a matter of just sitting a horse. Bob knew without vanity he could do that as well as most men. It was something new; not to be expressed. He had seen the deformed look of the gray's head straighten out as Bart drew near; the red flame of the eye die down. Bart had something on him—a new feel with a horse.

'I belong to the old school,' he muttered. 'All we know is that a hoss has to be broke; that a hoss is ruined that once gets his own way. Bart ain't a part of that. He makes a hoss forget his own way. He gives him his courage back. But it's disobedience—I dasn't let Bart get away with it. They'd think I was crazy—if I didn't get rid of the rat-tail.'

Mort Cotton took the old outlaw back to the Cup Q as a led-horse.

III

FINALLY the morning, a year or two later, when old Batten, the storekeeper at Bismo, was found murdered by Bob Leadley's serving woman who had gone over for a can of condensed milk. Her outcry roused the town. The old man had been hammered over the head and pulled out from his own back room, or else he had reached that far before they finished him. Things were spilled. There were sticky tracks on the floor and a winy smell in the gray of morning. A cask of apricot brandy in the place, no one knew how old, was still dripping when Bob Leadley got there. He recalled that Batten had never sold any of this brandy, holding it choice and sending a little flask to any one who was sick. What struck him queerly, too, was old Batten's thin white hair, not combed back as usual.

Letchie Welton came in and propped the old man up against the counter for a better look. The marshal's jaw got harder and whiter as he repeated that it was a Mexican job. The town was crowding in. Bob Leadley noted that his boy, Bart, was standing around. 'Go on back home and get your breakfast, Bart,' he said.

The whole white settlement was inside or at the store doors by this time. Mort Cotton's voice seemed to find the strangest hush for this sentence: 'They needn't have killed him. Old Batten would have given them all that they took—at least trusted 'em for what they took—'

It sounded so innocent and mournful, but it was like blowing on fire—the effect on the crowd. Every one was thinking something of the same kind, and a sort of hell took hold and united them—the same contagion that makes a mob. The cask had ceased to drip—not yet five in the morning. No one knew how much money Batten had in the place.

'A Mexican job,' repeated Letchie Welton, his jaw getting harder and whiter. 'We'll just go over to Dobe-town right now and see who's missing.'

They routed out the shacks across the river. Two Mexicans, Marguerin and Rueda, couldn't be accounted for; also a boy, called Palto around the diggings, was gone. About this time Bob Leadley noticed that Bart hadn't done what he was told, but had come over the stream with the rest.

'I told you to get out of here. Go home and wait till I come.'

Now Bob recollected that Bart and Palto had been thick at times.

No work on the mines that day. The 'Damask Cheek' filled early. Ten men chosen by Letchie Welton took the trail after the three Mexicans—a trail that showed clear—three ponies headed toward the Border, six or seven hours' start.

All were thinking, as they rode, of that old white head; ten men and the marshal, still keyed to that sentence which Mort Cotton had spoken. The thoughts of the posse working together this way made the purpose deadly. Each man grew painfully fond of old Batten, and the other side of the fondness was rising hate for the Mexicans ahead. Every little while some one said: 'Poor old Batten, he wouldn't have hurt a toad.'

They were several miles out, before Bob Leadley noticed that Bart was overtaking them from behind. At first he thought Bart was bringing a message from the town, but it proved he merely wanted to go.

'You turn around and ride back, just as fast as you can, young man!' the father said.

Those were the words which fixed it the other way.

'Let him stick. Good chance to see what he's made of,' Letchie Welton laughed, just as he would have said: 'Send him home,' if Bob had asked to let him stay.... The next day the posse was pressing the three Mexicans a lot closer. They didn't seem more than three hours ahead. It was desert work now, hot and grim. Toward nightfall, they came to a fork where the fugitives had broken apart, two turning to the left, one to the right. Letchie Welton sent four men after the lone pony to the right, and kept on with seven after the other two. On the third noon the two Mexicans, hard pressed, made their final split. This broke up the pursuing party a second time; Letchie Welton, Mort Cotton, Bob Leadley and Bart keeping on straight south, the other four turning east.

Toward sundown that third night, over a hundred miles from Bismo, only Bart was riding light and easy; his pony with a reserve left, the other three horses done for, and their riders as well. Canteens were empty; desert country, here and there a big solitary cactus, rising like a shade tree gone crazy.

'There's water ahead,' Bart told his father. 'I can tell by my pony's ears.'

The lower rim of the sun was out of sight when they came to the Mexican's horse, finished, lying at the edge of a pool of stagnant, coated water, choked in the hollows of a dry stream bed. The man-tracks stretched on toward a shadowy mass that proved to be the old hard-rock diggings of Red Ante, long since abandoned by any miners, Mexican or white. Letchie yanked up his horse's head from the pool.

'Our game's ahead, men. Come on, we'll get him and then come back to this pea-soup!'

Now, entering that deserted town, it was as if Bob Leadley had to see every detail. Not that he wanted to—but there seemed to be a pair of extra clear eyes, working back of his regular eyes, though he was partly out of his head from exhaustion. The abandoned street, between the huts of Red Ante, impressed him as something perpetual—moment and place. At the same time, a kind of insane anger was in his brain, because he had to hold up the weight of his horse's head on the bridle-rein. The beast with dying strength, was fighting to get back to that scummy pool; and Bob, a heap in the saddle, was needing all his strength to keep from falling. At the same time, those deadly clear eyes of his took in the bone-white curve of Letchie Welton's jaw, the big rent in Mort Cotton's shirt under the left arm toward the back, the skin showing wet and blistered there—and all the rest in that falling dark: Huts partly sunken in blowing sand—wide-open door of a deserted blacksmith shop—familiar as a lithograph that had hung in his room for years—wide-open door, rusty anvil, sledge standing by—big rusty bear-trap in the center of the dirt floor, with its half-inch chain running to the base of the anvil—everything sagging and dust-covered. Now Bob was letting himself down out of the saddle—when Letchie's pistol cracked, and his voice yelled:

'There he goes. I winged him. I got the son of—' A second pistol shot, as Letchie dug his spurs into his horse and pressed on the dark street. Bob Leadley and Mort Cotton staggered after him on foot, Bart keeping with them on his pony—to the last hut.

'It's Palto,' they heard the boy say.

The young Mexican was on the ground. The point dawning in Bob Leadley's brain was that it would have been so much better, simpler, if one or both of Letchie's shots had finished the job. Palto was down to pray— kneeling on the sand-blown, half-obliterated road. Welton jerked his horse so close, it looked as if he meant to trample the boy, before he stepped down. With his boot he shoved the figure over on its side.

'So it was you who did the hammering on old man Batten's skull—'

'Yo, no, señor!'

Not a man looking up, but the ashes of a boy—fag and fright all that was left.

'Weren't even there, were you? Home in bed all night. Just started out for a morning ride with Marguerin and Rueda—'

'Si, señor—was there, but no kill—'

Letchie turned his thin smile to the others. 'I guess you've heard that. I guess we've got what we came for. I guess we've heard from his own lips, he was one of the three.'

Bob Leadley wasn't right in his own head; he knew just enough to know that one thing. He saw his son looking down at Palto. He saw—a kind of humor about it—that Bart hadn't mixed in the pursuit with any sacred idea of the law's vengeance. Now the upshot of the whole matter from Letchie Welton:

'... accordin' to law, we can't finish him here and be done with it. Bein' still alive, we've got to fix to take him back to where a court is. Only if he should try to escape—we could put a bullet through him; but he won't do that, will you, Palto?'

'No, Señor!' sliding away from Welton's boot.

'We aren't the court and can't hang him here, and there's no shack in this hole of a town that will hold him. Our horses are done for—they won't get back to Bismo—'

Letchie's words died out of Bob Leadley's ears. He was trying to find himself. He was seeing old Batten's white hair, not combed as usual; he was seeing his own boy—a look in Bart's face, different from ever before. The hard white curve of Letchie's jaw was before his eyes and words again:

'I, for one, ain't sittin' up on guard to-night. I'm not askin' you fellows to do what I won't do myself.'

Something was crowding for utterance to Bob Leadley's lips, but Welton's voice kept it from coming clear. They might be here in Red Ante for days, while some one rode back to Bismo for fresh provisions and horses.

'... He ain't worth it—no greaser is. Only one way—to fix him so he can't get away—'

Now Bart spoke up: 'I'll stand guard over him to-night. I don't feel so done out—'

The father was glad in a crippled sort of fashion, glad but afraid.

'I guess not,' said Letchie. 'Wouldn't look so pretty when we got back, to have you tell 'em you sat rifle-up over the prisoner while we got our beauty sleep back.... No, I'm figurin' out a different way from what I saw up yonder—just as we broke into town.'

He meant the blacksmith shop. Bob Leadley saw Mort Cotton standing in the dark like a dirt-stained corpse. It might have been Batten himself.

'I won't take part in it,' Bob thought. 'I ain't marshal to say what's what, but I won't take no part.'

Bart was looking his way, but Bob didn't turn to meet his son's eyes. 'I ain't a man of law,' he was thinking. At the same time he felt Bart's eyes turning to him persistently, but he couldn't look. 'I ain't a man of law.'

The marshal was managing it alone....

Bob had been famished riding into town, but the stuff left in his saddle-bags tasted like worms to his tongue, and the water, as if running out of a sore. Though he was half dead for it, there was no sleep—with that racket from the blacksmith shop down the dirt road of Red Ante. He didn't meet Bart's eyes again. It was as if he had said good-bye to his son for life.

Bob had dragged his blankets away from the empty huts, far out on the sand to get beyond the cries, but they were already in his soul—no getting away. Long afterward, lying out there, he heard the sound of a single shot from the direction of the blacksmith shop—the end of all cries. Welton was there before him, Mort Cotton appearing from the side. Palto's troubles were over—Bart missing. It was not until daybreak that the father found a note pinned to his saddle—written by Bart before the shot had been fired.

I guess I don't belong here, Dad. I'll take Palto with me, if I can get him loose. Otherwise—well, you'll know. So long for good, BART.

I

THIRTY YEARS LATE

ARRIVING when the present century was well started, Elbert Sartwell had now concluded that his was a most untimely birth. For instance, all that war amounted to in his case, was the matter of wearing puttees to school. The magic of his youth was moreover smothered in a houseful of sisters— imprisoned in a sorority-house, he found himself—all his aching and persistent dreams unexpressed.

But the end had come. Elbert had reached decision; so had his father on the same point. They were at odds. It was a matter of grief to the son that for once there could be no compromise.

Fall darkness had closed about him, as these things appeared before Elbert's mind with finality. He left his room, followed the long wide hall to the door of his father's dressing-room and knocked. It was the last quarter of an hour before dinner, and the tone of the 'Come in' was not encouraging, but it didn't occur to Elbert to wait until dinner and tobacco had combed down his father's tag-ends of the day.

Mr. Sartwell was standing before his mirrors and did not turn, as the hall door opened. Elbert nodded at the reflection; also he observed in the glass a look of fresh vexation, which reminded him that his sister Nancy this very afternoon had smashed the fender and left front wheel of the new phaëton. His father had probably just heard about it. The present moment couldn't be worse, but Elbert didn't see how he could back out now with his ultimatum unreported.

'I've been thinking it over,' he said, 'and I can't start to work in the office, at least not now. You see, I've always wanted—'

'"Always wanted"—' broke in Mr. Sartwell, '"always wanted" against my better judgment.... A houseful of "always wanteds"! How can a man be expected to stand in the midst of six people, always wanting in different directions?'

'I hate to be an added trouble to you,' Elbert said in his unruffled way, 'but there's no use of my trying to go into the business, the way I feel.'

'What is it now?'

Still addressing the mirror, the younger man outlined with some embarrassment that he hadn't been able to get over his ardor to tackle life on a cattle range. The broad back before him suddenly jerked about. Elbert was held by the first direct look of one whose son has proved a definite disappointment. Many words followed; some heat:

'... pack a pair of pistols! Step along out over the real-estate ranges and prairie sub-divisions! Why, I'm actually ashamed to have to tell you, what any kid half your age knows—that there isn't a West any more, no cattle country—hasn't been for—why, you're only about thirty years late—' Also a final sentence, as Elbert withdrew, to the effect that if he did go forth, he would have to pay his own car fare 'out into the fenceless spaces.'

There was present at dinner that evening one of sister Nancy's young men friends, who had no dreams of the West whatsoever. The Sartwell family, diminished by recent marriages of two elder daughters, was pulling together socially, in spite of internal trouble. Elbert's thoughts were mainly afar on his own problem, but after a time, he couldn't help noticing the art with which the gentleman-guest played up to his father. It could be done, Elbert reflected. The two sons-in-law, already connected up, had also gone about it this way. He felt like a crossed stick; a spectator merely, in the home dining-room. His glance moved from face to face in the soft creamy light that flowed down through a thin bowl of alabaster, hanging from the ceiling. He alone, an only son, lacked a sort of commonplace craft to smooth his ways. He might have asked for a trip around the world before settling down to a business career—and gotten it.

Elbert retired to his room early. The Sartwell mansion faced the West, and sunsets had reddened his windows from as far back as he could remember. Long ago he had stared into a crimson foam of one certain day's end, thinking that it was the color of Wyoming. The lure of that crimson foam hadn't ceased, though it had moved farther South and farther West— Apache country, Navajo country—leading on over the border of late into Mexico itself.

He had been given an automobile at the end of high-school days, but he had wanted a pony. Hours at home he had spent in the garage, secretly wishing all the time it was a corral.

Elbert turned on the lights. Over the back of the chair he was sitting on, was a blanket of Indian red. There were framed Western drawings on the wall, paintings of rodeo and round-up, lonely cattlemen, bison, longhorns, desert and mountain scenes; and in among his books, pasted in an old ledger, was his collection of Indian pictures—heads of all the tribes, famous braves and medicine men—from cigarette, gum, candy packages—no end to the lengths he had gone to get the lot together. He looked back upon the time when the bronzed head of Red Cloud, of the Nez Perces, was the noblest countenance he had ever gazed upon.

A tall, cool person, Elbert could hardly remember ever being really tired. He was practically a stranger to all stimulants and dwelt altogether unaware in a calm that made nervous people either envious at once or hopeless altogether. His steady, homely hands were of that considerable size as to appear empty most of the time, and his blue eyes were so steady and cool that any one undertaking to go against his will, felt a surge of fatigue and irritation at the outset.

Elbert had been pondering a good deal of late on what sort of stuff he was made of. When he read of some hero's exploits in a newspaper, he asked himself could he have done that. And when he heard of some great suffering or privation of explorers, he wondered how he would have acted, had he been along. But it was the Southwest that perennially and persistently called. He moved to his phonograph, and picked out a book of records from the shelf below. The one he wanted wasn't there; in fact, he found it still in the machine, from a solitary performance of last evening—a Mexican record. He set it going now and a man's announcement in Spanish preceded the music, something about 'Paquita Conesa, tonadillera española, la mas famosa en Mexico y Sudamerica—'

... His favorite record. The song was 'La Paloma.' It always seemed to Elbert as if Señorita Paquita were singing in the open air. He smiled at a secret thought that always came to him, too—that the words of the song were carved out of starlight.

'Cuando sali de la Habana,

Valgame Dios—'

Up from the street, at the end of the song, reached his ears the tiresome sweep and swish of tires and carbureters, and from the drawing-room, Nancy's singing voice. Her young man would be standing beside the piano at this time, his waxen hair brushed back. Elbert smiled wistfully. 'Thirty years late.'

II

AT HEASLEP'S RANCH

FROM Kansas City, he sent his first letter back, regretting to leave home without talking it over further, but there didn't seem to be any use. Possibly there wasn't any more West, he allowed, but he had to go out and see. He hopped off the train at Tucson and heard of a stage that ran south toward the Border. That sounded right, and he walked three blocks with his bags to perceive—no jehu with long flicking lash, but a chauffeur, the stage being a motor-bus.

Elbert couldn't appreciate the scenery. Yes, there was a big ranch down yonder, the driver said. Yes, there was cattle. Irrigation and alfalfa had reclaimed this waste stuff. Some cows presently appeared wearing an 'HCO' brand.

'What does that stand for?' Elbert asked.

'Heaslep and Company.'

No Circle X or Lazy M—but irrigation, alfalfa fields, Heaslep and Company!

'The HCO runs everything down here—big land grant stretching almost to the Border,' the stage driver said.

Elbert was let down and made his way to a group of low buildings in the distance. At the farrier's shop, he inquired for the foreman, and was told to look for a door ahead, marked 'Office.' 'You'll find Frost-face in there or somewhere about,' the blacksmith said.

Elbert's pulse picked up a little at the name of the foreman, but it was certainly a business office he entered.

'We're not short-handed,' snapped the little gray man, with worried face. 'Things dull down in winter. Nothin' much to do right now but keep off the hoof-and-mouth disease.'

Outside there was a succession of sick blasts from a truck—the sound of an engine, not only decrepit, but dirty and dry. Elbert turned to the door.

'Wait a minute, young fellow. We might use a man on the chuck wagon—I wonder if you could drive old Fortitude?'

'A mule?' said Elbert. 'I'm sure I could learn—'

'Mule, hell, motor truck—can't you hear her?'

'I'm afraid I can,' Elbert said wearily. His father had been right.

One distinct value about Heaslep and Company, however—no women in the establishment. Even the cooking staff was Chinese. But the rest was hard to bear. Efficiency and trade had settled down as unromantically as upon a tannery. Heaslep's was a stock farm, a beef factory, anything but the cattle ranch of dreams. This part of Arizona was sunk in no foam of Indian red. The vast range lay on a squat mesa, partly penciled over with irrigation ditches. Elbert's tardy soul, longing for the thunder of a stampede, sickened at the sight of thousands of domesticated moos, rack-fed in winter, market-fattened from fenced alfalfa fields, branded in chutes and railroaded as scientifically as tinned biscuit. The only longhorns hung over the mantelpiece in the dormitory of the cowhands. Even the imported bulls were businesslike.

Most of the ranges were deserted by this time, the cold weather settling down. Elbert had been taken on as 'Bert' Sartwell, but his first letters from home gave the real thing away. All hands relished the discovery. Over a dozen of the men were in for his first Sunday, the day they started him in filling up gopher holes in the environment of the main buildings. Elbert was told that the best way was to soak old newspapers into a pulp and poke them down into the holes with a stick; necessary business every week or ten days during the gopher season. This was the height of it, he was informed.

'You see, the paper hardens down,' Cal Monroid said.

'And gets fire-proof,' added Slim Gannon, his side-kick.

Elbert set about his work, a bit coldish and blank at the extent of the job before him. He had never read of this department of ranch work, and wondered if it meant he was to be relieved of the motor truck. Toward midday he looked up from his poking, to find that at least ten of the cowhands had closed in, having stalked him like an Indian band. Their enthusiasm was high and prolonged. Elbert smiled and blushed, but said nothing. For a day or two after that they tried to call him 'Poke,' but the name didn't take hold. The men liked to say Elbert too well. 'Elber-r-rt,' they would chirrup, and inquire if he had ever done any bull-dogging.

He was not relieved from the truck. His work was to carry mails and bring in supplies from the town of Harrisburg, eleven miles to the north. He sometimes made two trips a day when the truck would permit, but the tantrums of old Fortitude were a subject of conversation at Heaslep's only a little lower in the scale than the hoof-and-mouth disease.

On his third or fourth Sunday, Elbert spread newspapers on the ground and set about taking down Fortitude's strained and creaking mechanism part by part. His activity and absorption began to attract a Sabbath crowd.

'He's gettin' her whole plumbin' out,' Slim Gannon remarked. 'I'm layin' four to three that we've heard her last belch.'

Cal Monroid considered for half a minute, noting the orderly lay-out of tools, inwards, greases and oils, and how carefully Elbert had numbered the parts. Cal began to fancy a vague purpose underneath it all and casually remarked: 'I'll just take you on, Slim, for half a month's pay.'

Elbert toiled through the hours. By sundown when he took his place at the wheel, all Heaslep's was taut with strain. The works purred, the car moved. 'It's down-grade, she's just rollin'!' breathed Slim. But Elbert reversed; old Fortitude backed and curved, did a figure eight to new music without hitting post or wall.

'I win,' said Cal.

'She ain't belched yet,' said Slim.

The two moved off to settle the technicality.

Dreary months of trucking. Elbert's insatiable interest in horsemanship had been little encouraged at Heaslep's. He was permitted to learn the bad ones by experience, and was rapidly disconnected several times, discovering his audience when it was too late, as on the day of 'poking' gopher holes. Though it was generally allowed things looked up a little when the range grass began to grow, Elbert lost heart before the winter was over. It seemed a long time to him since he had left home, but it wasn't so by the calendar. To judge by letters, the family had its hands out beckoning, but Elbert felt neither his father nor sisters would miss having the laugh at his expense.

Hard to leave Cal and Slim. This pair had warmed up a trifle toward the last. It was Cal Monroid who helped Elbert up from the turf the last time he was spurned by an HCO untameable, and Cal's easy tones had a soothing effect:

'It's about time you were sitting a real horse, Kid. Give me your shoe—'

And Elbert was lifted up on old Chester, who had his 'stuff' down so fine, you wouldn't believe he knew anything. Chester was the morning-star of Cal's string, and right then Elbert began to know the difference between an outlaw and a real man-horse. That one brief word 'Kid,' still sounded in his ears. It seemed to have let him into a new world, the world of Cal Monroid and Slim Gannon, the latter said to have taken the Tucson Bronk Cup two years straight; both men being held as cool and fast in a pinch. This episode held the faintest possible answer to what he had come West for, but Elbert had already decided to depart, his plan being to go on to the coast, before starting back East.

III

THE LEATHER-STORE

HIS first night in Los Angeles was like summer, though it was February. In the core of the old town he found the Plaza, and strolled through the Mexican crowd. His heart started a queer beat as the band struck up 'La Paloma,' his lips forming the words of the first line or two:

'Cuando sali de la Habana,

Valgame Dios—'

A wonder took him as to what Los Angeles used to be like when there were empty hills all around and how 'La Paloma' would have sounded in those days. 'Carved out of starlight,' he whispered.

The next day in the window of an old leather-store near the Plaza, he saw a cardboard sign reading: 'Young man wanted.' Elbert didn't suppose they would take on one without experience, but the impulse grew upon him to try his luck. The thought of going East so soon hadn't become any easier, nor did he consider with relish the idea of asking his father for money to stay away with. To his surprise he was given a trial in the leather-shop, and gradually he became pleased with the arrangement, for the store proved to have quality and background. Real cattlemen used to swear by it, he found out, and occasionally, even now, an old-timer would come in and talk with the proprietor. They would chat of the days when cantinas still welcomed the passer-by around the corner on North Main Street, little games going on upstairs. In those days the Mexicans hanging around the Plaza still had bits of color in their sashes and sombreros.

There was a gray wooden horse in the leather-store, fragile but full height, on which Elbert was accustomed to show bridles, saddles, blankets, and pack-gear, talking to customers a lot wiser than he felt, for he still resented life's conspiracy which had kept him from sitting a live horse where he belonged.

In the evening he would go out and lounge in the Plaza under the dusty palms and sycamores. It was better than Heaslep's in a way—the Mexicans had a friendly feel, and sometimes when the band played, he could imagine himself down in the City of Mexico, or in the heart of Sonora at least. One day during the dinner hour, when Elbert was alone, a calm-eyed, oldish man pushed ajar the door of the leather-store, looked slowly around and remarked in mildest tone:

'The first thing cow-people does, when they don't know what to do, is to saddle their pony.'

The voice was so gentle and leisurely, Elbert was warmed and interested at once. He was quite sure that nothing he could say about saddles would astonish such a customer, so he approached with a smile merely. The stranger had come to a halt before as fine a bit of workmanship in plain leather as the store contained.

'It ain't hem-stitched,' he began reflectively. 'Thirty-eight pounds.'

'Would you like to see it on the model?' Elbert inquired.

The other didn't seem to hear. 'Now, what would you expect me to lay out for a little tan kack like this?' he asked.

'Hundred-seventy-five,' Elbert said throatily. 'Would you like to look at it on the model?'

'No, it might confuse me a whole lot to see it on your dappled gray. Anyway, I can see Buddy Pitcairn made her from here. I'm shore partial about him monogram when I fork leather.'

A check was written with the remark: 'You can ship her to me, care of Mort Cotton's ranch at San Forenso, Arizona, and take plenty of time to look up this paper, young man. I never feel sure that the bank will like it, when I write out money for myself.'

The easy, rapid writing hinted an intelligence in curious contrast to the quaint speech and big loose hands, blackened and rounded to tool handles. The name on the check was Robert Leadley, and that was but the first of several calls which this customer made at the leather-store, ostensibly for further purchases, but always lingering to talk with Elbert. The latter had never known any one so easy to be with, and one late afternoon at closing time, when Mr. Leadley, with embarrassment, invited him to go out to supper, Elbert had been on the point of asking the same thing. They stopped for a soft drink at an old brown rail in Main Street.

'I 'member when this was a great sportin' place,' Mr. Leadley said. 'I used to come in here from the mountains with gold in a little chamois sack. Had a California claim in those days. I'm back in Arizona now, not a great ways from where I began. When the time came for me to go out this last trip, I felt like coming over to L.A., just like I used to from these mountains. Why, I was in this very place one night when a man was shot. Just yonder by that plate of hard-boiled eggs, he went down, callin' on a woman.'

'I didn't quite understand what you mean by "going out,"' said Elbert, not wanting to miss anything.

'When you've got a claim in the mountains and you figure on leaving, you designates it "going out."'

'Is it a gold mine?'

'Well, by stretchin' a trifle you might call her a gold mine—just a little claim by myself. Southeast a ways and high up. You go to San Forenso first. You can look back into California and down into Sonora from my diggin's.'

'Do you have horses up at the mine?' Elbert asked, thinking of the Pitcairn stock-saddle.

The quaint laugh sounded. 'Just a little vanity, young man. They do say Bob Leadley would have his saddle-hoss, if he was runnin' a canal boat. I can't seem to do proper without a bit of hoss-flesh handy, though Mamie sure costs me no end money and trouble, not bein' the sort of hoss as can pick her livin' off the north side o' trees—'

He paused, as if pleased to recall the mare to mind in minutest detail.

'Mamie's father was the stake-hoss, Ganopol—one of the first ten runners, they do say, and bone and blood to go with it, if not a whole lot of hoss-sense essential. Mamie's mother was just a cow hoss ... just a cow hoss, with a little clock workin' between her eyes—that was Clara. Thirteen years, I had her, and we got real domesticated together, you might say. Mamie's a five-year-old now—just about growed up—don't resemble neither parent none, bein' a jewel box by herself, full of her own little knick-knacks.... Yep, bred right out of the purple royalty on one hand and the black sage on the other, but approachin' my idea of saddle-hoss, plumb satisfyin'—

'An' p'raps it ain't such a chore, as I'm makin' out, to get hay and grain up to the mine,' Mr. Leadley added, 'because once or twice a year, Mort Cotton sends his mule train up from San Forenso to pack down my ore. Takes just about a week's work, three times a year, for a dozen or fourteen mules; and 'stead of the train pilin' back uptrail with empty riggin's, I stock up the cabin and the corral. Makes it easy, but a whole lot of times, I don't know where to put all I got—'

'But what do you do with your mare when you leave the mine?' Elbert asked.

'Leave her with Mort Cotton at his ranch in San Forenso. All hands have got to know her at Mort's.'

After supper they strolled back to the Plaza. The band began playing 'La Paloma.' Elbert started to speak, but Mr. Leadley's hand tightened on his knee for silence.

'I've got reason to remember that piece,' he said, when it was over. 'The Mexicans never get tired of it. It's like the Virgin speaking to them. Do you know what that word means?'

'Dove,' said Elbert.

'Correct. You must have studied the language?'

'Only the last few weeks. I'd like to know more. It would come handy in the leather-store. You know a lot about Mexico, don't you?'

'Not so much as I used to believe, young man, but I ain't averse to these people. I used to think I was, but as I look back now, I 'casionally catch myself wishin' I'd treated them as well as they have treated me. Just a curious feelin' at times—'

It didn't seem to be a deep matter to Mr. Leadley, his eyes were so pleasant.

'They're peaceful to be with, like cattle,' he went on. 'I lived on a farm back East when I was a boy, and my father and mother used to fight a whole lot—at supper, especially. I 'member often goin' out in the barnyard, and how peaceful it was, after the supper table. I don't mean Mexicans are cattle, you understand, only that they loll around and ruminate peaceful, like cattle.'

Elbert waited for more, and what came had a world of feeling in it that he didn't understand. It seemed the night was chillier, but the gentle tone hadn't changed.

'We used to call 'em greasers and shoot 'em up a lot, not thinkin' much about it. We used to hang 'em for hoss-thieves, when a sheriff wanted to make a showin'. Thought little more of 'em than a Chinee, only diff'rent. Young punchers and miners—we thought we was the people—'

The voice stopped so suddenly Elbert felt queer.

'You didn't tell me, why you have reason to remember "La Paloma,"' he said, looking across at the red lights of 'Estella Teatro.'

'I've got a boy about your size, I figure, somewhere south in Sonora—'

The words fanned to life the romantic pictures of Elbert's private world—'somewhere south in Sonora—'

'He used to like that song—used to whistle and sing it at all times. A dozen years since I saw him. He was under fifteen then—that would make him about your age now. You're pretty good size, but I think he'd show up a speck taller by this time.'

'What's your son doing down there?'

'Well, I only hear from him occasionally, through the papers. Must be excitin' work, having to do with the rurales, mostly. Some calls it politics in Mexico.... Maybe they'll play that again—if we sit down for a spell.'

And now Elbert was hearing the story of a boy, called Bart—no mother— life in a mining camp on the Rio Brava, Arizona—a sorry sort of helpless attachment in the father.

'The very night Bart came to town, before even the old Mexican nurse let me in, I knew my job was cut out,' Mr. Leadley said.

Sentences like these stood out in the midst of detail:

'I had everything mapped out for him, but he wouldn't follow the map. That broke me, because I mapped so hard and set so much store.... Bit by bit Bart showed me he'd have his way—taking his whippings easy, looking white, but ready to laugh, and going his own way just the same afterward. I never seemed able to do the right thing by him; couldn't let him alone; cared too much, I guess—the kind of care that hurts. Why, I'd get lonesome for him when he was right in the room, and flare up over things I'd never dream of getting sore about in any one else. Altogether, what I didn't know in them days was so much, young man, that I've been fillin' in ever since, and ain't through yet.'

IV

'ARE YOU DOOMED?'

AFTER they had parted, on the night of their first supper together, Elbert fell to thinking of his own relationships at home. This occupied him for an hour or two before going to bed—mixed in with memories of what he had heard about Mr. Leadley's missing son, and old days on the Rio Brava. He saw for the first time that there were two sides to this father-and-son business; that it was just possible a man might be able to talk to another man, saying things he couldn't tell his own son. Moreover, Elbert was able to see something of the tangle between Bart and his father with a clearness that had never come to him in regard to his own affairs.

He was a touch lonely that night, but queerly glad, for the first time, that he had never shown the knack to 'work' his father. All regret eased about that; better as it was.

Mr. Leadley didn't appear to be in any hurry to get back to his mine. It seemed to do him good to talk about the old days. Elbert listened eagerly, especially about Bart as a horseman.

'You see, he learned all we knew about hosses and all that the Mexicans know besides. He rode light, his hand quick, a sort of kidding way with him that got right into the good feelings of a hoss. I made him give up a bad one once and I had no right to do that, but I didn't see it straight until afterward. It was an old gray outlaw he brought home from a near-by ranch—a discard, but Bart was sitting him upright and amiable. That hoss pretty near finished me. I'm limpin' yet, on rainy days, from tryin' to correct his misdemeanors. And because I couldn't, it bore down on me not to let Bart ride him, who could. That was another mistake.... A hossman at ten, Bart was; had to have his six-gun before he was twelve. He could fan it, too. No use me tryin' to keep him from it, and the fellows I worked with at the mines whisperin' that he'd kill himself—that he wouldn't live to be hanged. You always hear what you're afraid of.

'Slim, black-haired, easy smilin' and Spanish on his tongue, Mexican spurs and reata, more interested in guitar music than gold mining, and off by himself or with the Mexicans instead of with his own kind. You know, Bart's mother was Spanish.... Yet any one could see Bart was game and gritty—life a feather to him—take it or leave it; laughin' but dangerous. No, they couldn't see it, either,' Mr. Leadley finished abruptly. 'I'm talking from a distance, from where I am now, I didn't see it myself then—not rightly, I didn't. I'm shore gettin' talkative.'

'I like to hear about him,' said Elbert.

'Now as to that, I had a queer feelin' you did from the first day I came to the leather-store. Guess that's why I've kept hangin' around—that, and your bein' about Bart's age and size.'

And yet, if it hadn't been for the curious sensitiveness within him that registered Mr. Leadley's feelings, Elbert would have thought that the other was merely recalling matters of pleasantness from years ago. Finally one evening, after talk touching Bart's prolonged stay below the Border, Elbert said:

'I'd certainly like to get somewhere down in Sonora.'

'Don't you ever draw a vacation at your store?'

Elbert laughed. 'I've only been there a few weeks.'

'I'd hate to cause any disaster in the leather business—'

'How do you mean?'

The other's voice became husky with strain. 'I was thinkin' as a starter, possibly, you might come over to my claim on your vacation.'

It began to appear more and more feasible as they talked. Directions opened right here at the Plaza. Elbert was told that an old friend and mining partner of Mr. Leadley's—Mort Cotton, now a cattleman, the same to whom the saddle had been shipped—would meet him at San Forenso and drive him up as far as the road went on the way to the mine.

'That's at Slim Stake Camp,' Mr. Leadley added. 'From there you just keep on hikin' up the canyon trail till you come to White Stone Flats, where I'll be watchin' for you—'

It sounded somewhat complicated to Elbert. 'But suppose I should miss the trail?' he said.

'I can't see how you could, unless you got headstrong—'

'But how am I to know when I get to White Stone Flats?'

'By composin' yourself to listen a little longer. First you see two big pines less'n twenty feet apart, still alive, but showing marks of a forest fire ten or twelve years back.'

'I'm afraid I wouldn't know how a tree would look, twelve years after a forest fire—'

'Right, you wouldn't, but that ain't all to go by. It is a Flats, remember, and on the Flats is a lot of big white stones, and printed on the biggest of 'em in black letters, "ARE YOU DOOMED?"'

Elbert saw himself getting there.

'... humorist—now I wonder?' Mr. Leadley went on. 'Or just a pious gent coming up into Nineveh, as if sent for? "Are You Doomed?"—he paints, right on the big stone facin' the trail, and a little ways off on a smaller stone, he fixes the answer: "JESUS SAVES." That there handwritin' on the rock seems to be for me, 'cause every time I go for water—there it is. But as I was sayin', you'll know you're comin' to the Flats when you get to the last water.'

'How shall I know it's the last water?'

''Cause pretty soon after that you'll come to the Flats. Anyway, I'd be watchin' on the day set—'

Elbert was finally able to arrange a few days off, without losing his job outright, though he felt queerly uncertain about coming back, the claim being beyond Yuma on his way East. On a morning in late March, he reached San Forenso, where he was met by Mr. Cotton, with a two-horse rig. The hand that Elbert gripped was crippled in shape, but did not lack strength, and the eyes of Mr. Leadley's old partner peered into his with such frequency and deep intent from under their bushy white brows, that Elbert began to feel he had never before been so exhaustively appraised.

'Has Bob started in tellin' you about Red Ante, yet?' Mr. Cotton asked after they had driven some time.

'No,' said Elbert, wondering if Red Ante were a game.

'Now that's funny—he never gets away from that when I see him. That's one reason I don't see him a whole lot more. Told you about Bart, of course—'

'Yes.'

'Way back in Bismo—'

'Yes—'

'And stopped short at Red Ante?'

'I didn't hear him mention—'

'Now that's queer—nothin' about a man not bein' able to wash his hands?'

'No,' said Elbert, more mystified.

'Can't be it's dyin' out of him,' Mr. Cotton mused, eyes rigid on the flanks of his team, as they wound up a canyon trail. 'But that ain't the kind of thing as dies out,' he added.

At Slim Stake Camp, where the road ended, Mr. Cotton excused himself to write a note to Mr. Leadley, which Elbert was asked to deliver. 'And don't let him fill you up none on how bad he's treated Bart,' was the last swift injunction. 'I was along myself in them days and I didn't miss all that was goin' on.'

Elbert nodded attentively.

'Remember what I say, when he starts tellin' you about Red Ante!' shouted Mr. Cotton, holding hard on his swerving team.

A while after that Elbert was alone on the steep canyon trail, his ears cracking like drying wallpaper from the altitude, and his heart windily at work. Springs saturated the earth from time to time. There positively didn't seem to be any last water, until the trail widened in mid-afternoon and there faced him:

'ARE YOU DOOMED?'

White Stone Flats. He found the two pines that had lived through the fire—all straight, but no Mr. Leadley to meet him. He called a little, but the raising of his voice left him queerly uneasy. There was food in his roll, and he finally spread his blankets and stretched out for the night. The idea struck him that he must soon get back to work, for it seemed like ten days already.

Mr. Leadley must have forgotten the date. Up here anything was possible. Hours after, a white glare through the eastern trees and a tardy, bulging moon showed up; then quite the most curdling wail sounded through the whitish night. It was 'doggy' in depth and volume, but the wauling of it was like a greatly enlarged cat. Now Elbert had an opportunity to study the stuff he was made of. He wasn't encouraged. His heart was knocking to get out. Nothing short of a mountain lion made that noise.

There was another sound—hard to place, that welled out of the dragging hours—a queer hum, so soft that one didn't know whether it was a mile away or in his hair. It was like a woman going insane, but not violently.

Hard to believe, but the sky began to show signs at last that another day was actually to be given to mankind. Elbert was making coffee in full daylight, when another outcry reached him—his first dawning suspicion as to the human quality of these tones. He stood up; his hand actually shook as he set down his tin cup, and his eye caught the black letters:

'ARE YOU DOOMED?'

'How did you know?' he muttered—and right then, the call again—vaguely like his own name. A minute later he was running across the Flats, his ears verifying as he ran:

'Oh, Sartwell—this wa-a-ay!' ahead, and somewhat above.

'Yes, I'm coming!'

On the easy slope before his eyes, he saw a trail.

'... turn to the left at the rotted cedar!'

The voice nearer, his own steps soundless for sixty or seventy feet along the punk of fallen timber; then a bald ridge which the winds had swept clean—a hand raised from the gravel—the old man crumpled there, his lips stretched white in a pained smile.

'A long time gettin' to you ... couldn't make it last night. Where's your canteen?'

'Back with my stuff—shall I get it?'

'No, I guess I can wait a little longer. We'll get to the cabin. Mebby, leaning a whole lot, I can walk a bit.'

'What did you do? You haven't been lying out here all night?'

'Yes. It happened in the tunnel yesterday 'bout noon—falling rock ... too big for the small of a man's back. Started a trickle in there, somewhere—'

Did he mean in the mine or in his back?

'Left me uncoupled. Too bad to spoil that vacation of yours this way.... Figured I could reach you by crawlin'—but played out—couldn't make you hear in the night. Feared you might have gone back to town.'

Mr. Leadley couldn't stand now, even with help. Elbert shouldered him at last; a long hard pull up to the cabin. No need for directions the latter part of the way, for a horse kept up an incessant nickering—like showers of gold coins falling upon a metal surface.

'That's Mamie. She ain't been fed since yesterday mornin',' the old man apologized. 'She never misses bestowin' her welcomes, though it ain't like her to be quite so noisy. She's a real listener, too, Mamie is.'

A cabin in the midst of a group of great yellow pines. Elbert entered the open door, gasping with his burden. The old man's tortured mouth still smiled up at him from the bunk. The room smelled like cigar-box wood. It was stuffed with chests, cupboards and cabinets—a hand-hewn room, with massive frame and heavy cedar shakes on the outside. Elbert brought water and started to unlace the nearest boot.

A ghost of the old chuckle and the words:

'No, nothing for me, 'til you go feed Mamie. She ain't used to bein' treated like this—'

Half in a dream, Elbert went out to the little corral, lifting the wooden pin that let him in. The mare played curiously about him, but mainly kept her eyes to the cabin; her ears straight out for a voice from there. He only saw a bay butterball at first—shiny satin in the bright sunlight—a lot more rounded out than the wooden horse in the leather-store, not so tall as Cal Monroid's Chester, which had stood in Elbert's mind up to this moment as all that a horse could be.

He was thinking of the look he had seen in Bob Leadley's face; and of the rock, too big for the small of a man's back, and of feeding the mare before anything could be done. He dropped a measure of grain into the manger under the shed roof, but Mamie didn't stay with it. She kept running up and down the corral, nickering softly, listening, her head cocked toward the cabin, her ears held forward pointing to the open door. She seemed appareled in sunshine.

V

'I, ROBERT LEADLEY—'

THAT leak wasn't in the mine.

'I feel a trickle inside, young man—'

Thus, every little while, through the heat of the day, the old man intimated his hurt, and how he felt himself bleeding internally. Elbert's idea was to set out at once and in a hurry to bring help from Slim Stake Camp, but Mr. Leadley so far had persistently refused to let him go.

'Things I've got to say are more important. You never can tell when I'm apt to start talkin'—don't go yet. I'm restin' a little first, that's all—'

When he dozed, Elbert roamed about outside, but within call. Everything imaginable in the way of canned goods, dried fruits, preserves, were stored in a shed as commodious as the cabin; ample supplies of tobacco, quantities of unused tools. Stocked for a year, the place looked; with at least a ton of baled hay and many bags of grain in the corral-shed. All the carpenter work was made of cedar; hand-tooling everywhere—work of a man who liked to bring out the best with a sharp blade; quaint art about the cabinets and wooden insets in the fireplace.

Down trail to the right from the cabin door was the tunnel entrance to the mine, and ahead out over many tree-tops, a glimpse of the Flats, in a great pit of saffron light. Elbert kept thinking he should go for help in spite of Mr. Leadley's protestations. A call from the cabin hurried him in shortly after noon.

Twice the injured man's lips started, before he got words going:

'Maybe I ain't goin' to die, and maybe I am. That's all right—only there's some things I mean to say first. It wasn't only a vacation I brought you here for—that and somethin' else, though I didn't expect to be hurried like this, in unburdenin' my mind. Yes, sir, I took to you the minute you looked so inquirin' as to what I meant, when I came in that leather-store ... same age and all that, as Bart down in Sonora—and when you hints you'd like to get down there .... Draw up a box to write on, and bring me a little leather sack of papers in the lower cabinet by the fireplace—the key in the wallet here. You're to write down what I say.'

Reserves of will-power were drawn upon; part of the quaint twang went out of the old man's speech:

'I, Robert Leadley, of the Dry Cache mine, near San Forenso, Arizona, in sound mind, so far as I know, but badly hurt from a fallen rock in the tunnel of said mine—my own fault because I knew for a long time there were spots that needed timbering—do hereby confer upon my young friend, Elbert Sartwell, who is writing this at my word, the sole right and authority to manage and administer all property I possess—'

Elbert had no chance to interrupt. The enumeration went on without a break, including the Dry Cache mine, saddle-horse, all goods stored in cabin and corral-shed, bank-books, documents and keys to a lock-box in the San Forenso Bank—amounting to about ninety thousand dollars, Mr. Leadley explaining that he had refused an offer of seventy-five thousand dollars for the mine itself.

'Don't sell in a hurry,' he broke in. 'There's a gold tooth in her head. Mort Cotton understands. You can tell that to Bart—'

'I tell Bart—'

'That's the general idea—'

'But how do you mean, Mr. Leadley?'

'Because Mort Cotton can't go—I've talked to him—and administerin' property isn't his line. It's—it's because I took to you—that's the main reason. Listen on—let me get it all out straight.'

Gradually it appeared that Mr. Leadley's desire was to leave the bulk of what he possessed to his only son, Bart Leadley, now somewhere in Sonora, Mexico, at large, and Elbert's work to find same. Elbert was to be identified by Mr. Cotton who would help him through business of bank and possible probate, and answer all questions as to why the property could not be left and arranged for in the usual way. A generous salary and expense account was provided, and on the day Bart Leadley was brought back to the States, Elbert was at liberty to assign to himself a one-fifth interest in the Dry Cache mine; a second one fifth to go to Mort Cotton, memo of which was on separate paper, and three fifths to the son, Bart Leadley.

Elbert's eye was held to the page, after this was written, his mind so lost in what it all meant, that the voice from the bunk actually startled after a silence:

'Well, how about it, young man—does the paper stand?'

'But—in case your son isn't to be found—at least, from anything I can do?'

'All you have to do is convince Mort Cotton of the facts, and the whole business then lies between you and him. There's nobody else.'

Elbert went to the door to breathe, more astonished than ever before in his life; astonished and hurt, too, by the reality of this friendliness, and the mystery of the smiling courage with which Mr. Leadley bore his pain. Sonora—to find Bart Leadley at large in Sonora—expenses to draw from— an interest in the mine. His eyelids narrowed as he turned from the corral, where the mare stood listening in the vivid afternoon light.

Then presently he saw, stretched from one branch of scrub-oak to another, between him and the corral gate, a shining thread that hung and waved in the sunlight. Just a spider's suspension cable, but a deep meaning now about that connecting thread; so thin one wouldn't see at all, if the sun hadn't been shining just right. Mr. Leadley had trusted him, felt drawn to him, even before the accident in the shaft—mysterious threads binding people together. Why, that must have been the meaning of his taking the job in the leather-store. The voice called from behind:

'But Bart Leadley isn't dead! I don't feel he's dead,' Mr. Leadley said, when Elbert hurried in. 'No, you won't be able to go for a doctor just yet—little later for that, maybe. The paper's done, but there's something to tell about Red Ante before you go—and, yes, about Mamie. I'm giving her to you outright, not that Bart isn't a horseman—he's that before everything else— but you might be a long time findin' him, and I don't want her to change hands too often. And then you're the one who'll need her in Sonora.... Don't try to run her, young man. Just try to come to an understanding. Stand around and talk to her—she's one more listenin' mare. She likes to be consulted about family affairs. It won't do you no harm. And don't ever tie her up, when you camp in the open. She'll graze within range and keep an eye on you besides, like her mother used to. You'll get the hang of each other. Keep on her right side, and whistle when you want her—'

He put two fingers to his lips to show how. Elbert couldn't make a sound that way. He thought of getting a whistle to carry.

As dusk thickened, a wind stirred across high country—sometimes the sound of a waterfall, sometimes the sound of the sea in the top branches of big timber. The mountains grew heavy on Elbert's heart with the falling night. Meanwhile he was encouraged to bake a honey-cake for his own supper.

'No, you don't need salt nor sodie—all that's in the flour—just can-milk and honey in the batter, an' grease on the pan.... Not too near the coals, an' keep turnin' her round and round. You'll have a cake yet, young man, and what you have over you can feed Mamie to-morrow. She'll like it, if it's good.'

'Just a trickle—'

Elbert heard the words from time to time through the first half of the night. Then for a while delirium was unmistakable:

'*You didn't have to go, Bart*—' the voice once said in a wistful tone, and names were uttered with dread, yet a kind of life-long familiarity as well: 'Welton—Letchie Welton.' ... 'Palto' ... 'Mort Cotton' ... 'Red Ante' and in and out through sustained incoherencies, with dreadful impressiveness, references to a blacksmith shop: and once starting up, the old man found Elbert's eyes and spoke slowly with intolerable contrition:

'*There are times when you can't wash your hands, I'm sayin'. It wasn't what I did—but what I didn't do?*'

Toward daylight he slept, but it was only for an hour or so. Elbert, drowsing in a chair, heard the call.

'Start some coffee for yourself, and turn in a measure of grain for Mamie; then draw your chair close. You'll be goin' down trail for a doctor this morning—I know it's bearin' heavy on you, and maybe there won't be much talkin' after the doctor comes.'

Altogether quiet and hasteless—so different from the delirium of the night. It was dim and cool in the cabin; the sun not yet over the ridge; fragrant firelight, coffee on to boil.

'You can telephone Mort, too, from the lower camp. He wouldn't like it, if I didn't let him know, and bring your coffee here.... Yep, sit in close.'

At times it seemed as if the old man were easing a burden from his heart, as gradually Elbert began to get it all straight: The mining town of Bismo, Arizona, one morning twelve years ago; an old storekeeper, murdered in the night—young Bart hanging around, though sent back—Bart following the posse and being permitted to stay by the marshal when they were ten miles out.

Elbert had to be reminded of his coffee as the story of the three days' chase carried on—hunger, thirst, fatigue: how one of the Mexicans split, breaking up the pursuing party also—Letchie Welton, Mort Cotton, Bob Leadley and his son Bart continuing straight south, four others turning east. Then it was that the telling took on an unprecedented intensity, though the voice was held low.

'Over a hundred miles from Bismo, and just before dark, coming to water and an abandoned town called Red Ante. Bart ridin' light and easy; the rest of us done for, my horse dyin' under me, ears loppin', the weight of his head hangin' on my arm. I'd ridden him to death—that made me all the uglier.... Gettin' dark, as I say, and we halted at the edge of that dusty hell-hole, everything saggin' and sand-blown.... Palto—our work wasn't over—'

'But what did they do to him?' Elbert burst out a moment later; yet he was afraid to hear. The cabin interior had taken on a startling unreality. He seemed to be back in Red Ante ... the lone sandy road that nightfall twelve years ago. Then the quiet words:

'Recollect what I told you was in the blacksmith shop?'

Elbert moved to the door, his eyelids narrowed by the sunlight. He was ill, intolerably shaken, but the weary voice followed him.

'I know it ain't pleasant to hear, young man. It ain't been pleasant to live through—that night, nor for a dozen years. It don't get no better, but you've got to know. And there's only a little more—'

Elbert braced for the rest. What called his will-power to bear it was that he was only listening to a story a dozen years later, and this man had lived through the action of it—had heard the sounds—had lost his boy—just a note pinned to the saddle, all that was left.

The old man turned his face away.

'I guess that's about talk enough from me right now,' he said after a moment, 'only that when we got back to Bismo, they entered a murder charge against Bart. 'Mebbe it was murder Letchie,' Mort Cotton said at the hearin', 'but the most merciful bullet I ever heard fired, was that one of Bart's just 'fore he rid out of Red Ante.' But no words of Mort's or mine did any good.... You can go down trail now. Mort'll tell you the rest, if I don't get to it—'

VI

THE LISTENING MARE

TWO weeks later Elbert was closing up the cabin. He had been through all the papers. There was one having to do with the lineage of Ganopol, a running horse, with lines tracing back to Europe and the Near East, and the days when man and horse were mates of the world. Names—feminine names of the desert like those of the Old Testament, for the horse-lines of Araby were kept from mother to daughter and not from father to son— 'The Listening Mares.' There were sweet meadow names of England ... there was a remark in pencil on one corner of the big sheet:

'Her pedigree isn't any longer than a piece of burnt string, and where she got herself from, I'm not prepared to state, but for a horse to sit on and come across with good sense, little Mamie's mother, old Clara, was sure a triumph of breeding—'

It was almost like a voice. Elbert turned his eyes to the empty cot. It was as if he could see Mr. Leadley looking over the certificate of registration and writing down that remark—not having any one to speak aloud to. A lot of talk about Mamie's father—too much silence about old Clara, he had probably thought. A little later as Elbert touched a match to some papers in the fireplace, these brief but laborious lines caught his eye:

'... On looking him over at your request, Bob, I don't feel troubled about his honesty, but I'm not so sure he's real bright.'

It was the letter he had brought up trail from Mort Cotton that first day at San Forenso. Another proof that Mr. Leadley had been thinking of sending him down into Sonora for Bart, before the accident in the shaft. He had asked his old partner's judgment. This reminded Elbert of Mr. Cotton's first fierce appraisal of him in San Forenso. A low nicker reached him from the corral and a flushed smile came to his face, as he moved out.

Somehow in lifting the wooden pin of the cedar gate, the sense came over him again of the quality of the man whom he had known so well—just a pin of manzanito to hold the gate, but there was an art about the way the knots were cut. The mare came up to him nodding and stepping high with her front feet. She seemed to say that this conspiracy to keep her in the dark had gone far enough; that the time had come for her to know what was going on.

'... And you're to be mine, Mamie—from now on!' Elbert muttered. He had been trying to get used to it for days. 'What do you think about that? Not very much, I guess.... Not much more than Mort Cotton did, probably.'

The mare wasn't telling. She was friendly, however, nudging under the arm, nosing at his hands and pockets.

'Oh, I know what you want—a piece of cake.'

He went back to the cabin. The strangest feeling came over him in the shadows. This was his place to come and go in, but the fact was slow to settle in him. He missed his old friend and didn't feel quite up to the reality of possession. One man's whole life—these things represented—and a mare that couldn't be bought.... There might have been some hope, the doctor had repeatedly suggested, if Mr. Leadley could have been moved down to San Forenso, but the old man had refused to hear to that. He had to come to his own conclusion, apparently. Days of just sitting around— Mort Cotton there, the doctor riding up to the claim every day—about as hard days as the young man had lived through so far.

The last chest was locked, the last cabinet.

Elbert glanced around before shutting and padlocking the outer door of the cabin—a wonder passing through him about sometime coming back—with Bart.... In a sense, this meant his start for Sonora right now. Of course, there were matters to close up in San Forenso—affairs of the Dry Cache, of banks, papers and probate, but Mamie was now to be ridden down trail and it was like the beginning of a new life. From the doorway, he studied the mare's sculptured head. There she stood, as if listening to sounds which she alone could detect.

Practically his first experience in saddling anything but the wooden horse. The horses he had failed to tarry on at Heaslep's had been saddled by others—even old Chester on that unforgettable day. He knew the straps and cinches—part of his recent business, and Mamie wasn't too restive, so far. Funny, Elbert thought, that he should have sold that Pitcairn stock-saddle to himself, after all.

'Thirty-eight pounds,' he muttered.

Trouble came to Mamie's eyes as he undertook to tuck the steel between her teeth. She didn't like the way he went about it; also it seemed, he had to mash her ears about to get the bridle on. She was nervous as a child being severely washed. Finally the man got his foot in the stirrup and raised himself. With a little dance to the right, the mare glided from under, and stood with trailing bridle-rein, looking at him, confused and incredulous.

'I guess I couldn't have stepped up on her in the way she's used to,' he remarked.

He tried again. Mamie seemed to have a certain responsibility for him this time, like a mother-hen trying to get on with an unfamiliar chick. But she had her own mysterious forces and impulses to cope with, too. She had been penned-in for altogether too many days and darted out of the corral gate with a suddenness that jerked the man's body and arm back to keep his place. Mamie's head flung upward in utter dismay, and the awfulness of having put weight like that on her tender mouth, uncentered Elbert entirely for the time. It was like clashing gears in a fine machine that has been desperately hard to obtain—only ten times—infinitely worse—this, a living thing, cherished from a baby by an old man who had been a horseman all his days.

The saddle kept slipping forward. Elbert hadn't known at first how to tighten the girths. He didn't dare to look underneath. At least, there was no blood mixed with the foam around the steel of her bit.... Twenty-two miles down trail, and long before the end, his own agony took the edge of strain from the fierce imaginings of damage he was doing the mare. Mamie didn't stop to walk; she danced down trail—to friends of hers at Mort Cotton's ranch. It was as if she expected, when she got there, to hear the voice that had been silent so long. A hundred times Elbert thought of this. His bones crunched; he felt the scald of blood and sweat on his thighs. But once or twice, even in the pain, a flash of splendor went through him—at her arched lathered neck, the lift of power from beneath, some new magic from the earth—

No need to ask the way to Mort Cotton's place. Mamie veered to the left, at the end of San Forenso's main street, following the wagon tracks at a show-trot to the wide gateway, where she was welcomed from all quarters at once. Mort Cotton called his greeting from the doorway of the ranch house, as Elbert let himself down, steadying himself before letting go of the pommel. Mort approached. What was left of the younger man withered as those eyes, under the white bushy brows, fixed upon the mare. This was far more severe than being appraised himself.

'Lucky old Bob couldn't see her, with the saddle as far back as that,' Mr. Cotton remarked.

Elbert had ceased to breathe. Raw and angry patches wavered in imagination before his eyes, as the saddle was being removed. Hide and hair unruffled—a flood of thankfulness went through him. He moved around to Mamie's far side and all looked intact there, too. Mort's twisted hand was now knuckling down the buttons of the mare's spine.

'Thought so, all the weight on her kidneys. Say—' The old man's glance had turned to Elbert really for the first time, the sharp eyes settling upon his riding cords. 'Caked, or I'm a Spaniard! I see you've been punished, too. Come on into the house. The boys will take care of Mamie. They know her.'

Elbert obeyed, but made no move to a chair as they entered the cool front room.

'I led her down part of the way,' he confessed unsteadily. 'But she wanted to get here. She's so much—all the time—'

'She sure is—so much hoss all the time. I know her. And what you want now, young man, isn't to hurry away nowhere too sudden, but quarters to cool down in right here, good upstandin' quarters. And say, I've got some hosses for you to do your rough ridin' on. Mamie's a bit too fine to break a man in. I'm goin' to give you some lessons personal, before you leave, and bring you up, so's you'll know what you're ridin', when you get Mamie under the saddle—'

'Not at once,' said Elbert.

'No, you'll be walkin' like a bear for a week yet.'

VII

THE SOFT SIDE OF A SADDLE

ELBERT limped out to Mort Cotton's stables next morning. Mamie saw him coming, her head hanging out above the half-door. She began nodding in a way that made him know she was pawing the ground, though he couldn't see her feet. It wasn't hay she wanted. Was it word of the one who did not come, or more of the Road, she was asking for? Elbert wouldn't have confided to any one the humility he felt, as he moved close. All through a painful night, he had dreamed of the mare running from him, fighting his approach and presence. She would stand up on her hind legs and strike at him when he came near. Ugly lot of sleep torments, in which Mamie was always getting hurt—his fault—but nothing to them after all. Here she was fresh and blithe as usual, nudging, nosing, ready as a child to begin all over again. A fine lift went through him, that she didn't hold a grudge.

He had to rub his eyes after a moment ... Mexico, riding South, plazas at night, camps in the open, days in the saddle, the freedom he had dreamed of.

... In the next ten days all business was finished in San Forenso and Elbert was healed enough to begin his course in horsemanship under Mort Cotton—the actual riding part. So far as words went, the drill had begun at once.

'What you need is hardenin', young feller, and that comes gradual. You've been sittin' on cushions all your life and a stock-saddle ain't like that. The soft side of a stock-saddle is placed next to a horse. You got to learn to fit to it, because it's made not to give. After that, you've got to learn to ride easy. It ain't like sittin' on a box in a grocery store. You can always tell a man with no sense to a horse, sitting up and takin' it for granted, that a horse is meant to carry him. A man's weight's got to be alive—part of his horse—not a dead weight like a pack-mule carries. Bob Leadley used to say a good deal at the last that there's plenty of good "riders" but only one in a hundred real horsemen.'

'I've heard him say that,' said Elbert. Times like this, he wished Mort Cotton wouldn't stop. The old cattleman was altogether unlike Mr. Leadley, but the two had been so much together, that a feeling of closeness to Bart's father came to him as he talked and rode with Mort. There was much still he needed to know about the old days.

'... I wasted a lot of time hatin' Letchie Welton,' Mort Cotton once said. 'But there's no good in that. Old Bob found that out, too. You wouldn't fancy him a fightin' man, but I saw him flare up. Letchie Welton can thank me that he lived for Lon Bimlock to kill him. It was at the hearin' back in Bismo, and Letchie was tellin' our fellow townsmen that he had a suspicion right at the beginning that Bart was in with the other three in the murder of old Batten. That, he said, was why he insisted on Bart bein' allowed to ride on with the posse—so he could watch him. As it happened Bart got away. No question in his mind, Letchie Welton gave down at the hearin', but that Bart had killed Palto to prevent him squealin', before ridin' out to connect up with his share of the loot. "Didn't he want to stay up all night in order to let Palto go free?" Letchie wanted to know.... As I say, I had my work cut out to keep old Bob from killin' our deputy sheriff that day.

'... No, sir, we weren't exactly right—never have been, Bob and me, since that night in Red Ante,' Mr. Cotton observed, another time. 'They talk of shell-shock these days. It wasn't shells that got us, but we were shocked men just the same. It worked this way: We never could stay long where men were—never could get along in the settlements any length of time. We took up prospectin' to get up into the mountains alone, but we couldn't be too close, even to each other, for very long. I've seen Bob go apart to smoke of an evenin', after we'd worked separate ridges all day, and I've felt the same way. It was quite a while before we came to know we were so different. I began to see it in Bob, and gradually it worked out that he could see it in me.

'I wouldn't have believed it of Bismo, and Bob couldn't, but that town wasn't wrought up over what happened in Red Ante, like we were. Seems as if Bob and me took the full shock of that, though we were slower catchin' on, than young Bart was. Palto's bein' a Mexican seemed to make it all right for Bismo. A greaser had murdered a white man and a whole Mexican village of men, women and children couldn't pay for that.... Always a man of law, Letchie Welton was. Bismo called him a trail-burner for bringin' in his man, and made him sheriff afterward. He held his job until three or four years back when he was shot from his horse, as I told you, on the trail of Lon Bimlock. They say Letchie was sleepin' his last sleep before he touched ground that day, havin' taken Lon's forty-five between the eyes.'

There was a lot of inexpressible feeling in Elbert's chest as he listened to certain observations of Mr. Cotton on the relationship between Bob Leadley and his son. It made him draw a step nearer that mystery of mysteries, his own father. 'Bob was a strong man with men before Bart came,' Mort once said. 'Then gradually on that one point they came to think of him as the favorite fool of the diggin's. Some said he was too easy, some said he was too hard, but all said he was wrong.

'... But I was tellin' you about the last days in Bismo. You see Bart couldn't come back if he had wanted to. It got worse against him as weeks passed and Marguerin wasn't brought in. Rueda was caught and hung, his last words bein' that Marguerin had done the killing. Word reached Bismo that Marguerin and Bart were together in Mexico, ridin' with Monte Vallejo, who was just a bandit-leader down in Sonora in those days, but high up in Sonora politics right now—apt to be the big gun if the Government turns over. Also we've heard various times that Bart is still ridin' with Monte Vallejo—that's one of the things Bob must have wanted you to know.

'Bob was down in Mexico five years back and might have come up with Bart, except as he tells it, all at once the rurales began to take an interest in his case. They couldn't do enough to help him find what he was after. You see the rurales are a strong body of men, workin' sort of alone-like, mainly on the side of the Government, and hell-bent after all bandits, when they feel like it—'

'How did the rurales find out what Mr. Leadley was down there for?' Elbert asked.

'Now as to that, my mind's at rest. Letchie wasn't done for at that time. He tipped 'em off, as I see it—always a man of law, Letchie was. And, of course, the rurales would be interested in a white man down there, lookin' for his son who was said to be ridin' with Monte Vallejo, for the rurales have been tryin' to get their hands on Vallejo for years, but you see the common people like the big bandit, and are not so strong for the rurales, who lord it over 'em and feel important, havin' the law on their side.

'Old Bob always kept track of Monte on Bart's account. He used to bring me translations from the Mexican papers, how Monte had burned this, and beaten his way through that, and how the rurales had just missed capturin' him. If I was you, I wouldn't try to cross the Border straight down from here. Ride east for three or four days, takin' your time and make your crossing at Nogales. You'll be able to get in there, more quiet and unwatched, and you're more apt to be closer to the scene of operations of the man you're lookin' for. It won't be long before you'll be hearin' of Monte Vallejo's doings. He's 'specially active right now. If Bart's still with him—that's another thing. Anyway take it easy, an' take your time—'

'I know that road south of Tucson to Nogales worked at Heaslep's drivin' a truck,' said Elbert, 'I might stop off for a day or two to see a couple of friends of mine—'

'So long as you don't tell anybody what you're out on,' warned Mr. Cotton. 'I'm sure Bob would have advised you this way—if he'd had time.'

'I'll be careful about that,' Elbert said, and yet his pulse pricked up at the thought of another sight of Cal and Slim.

VIII

HEASLEP'S AGAIN

HE was actually on the Road, traveling east toward Tucson, Mamie showing up from hour to hour a little better than he could ask or expect. Elbert had to keep telling himself that there was no hurry, no stress, but the urges of all past years rose up in him, trying to make him believe that everything was ahead, instead of here and now.

Expense money to work with, a gold mine back of him; best of all, there was a purpose to carry out; a meaning back of his setting forth. Had he tried to plan it all before leaving the East, he couldn't have arranged an adventure half so satisfactory as this—not just an aimless ride, no mere purposeless freedom. By some marvelous destiny he had come into the right to venture forth—a quest to work toward, an allegiance to make good with Mr. Leadley and his son, with silence on his tongue all the way.

No, he was not to tell any one—not even Cal and Slim, if they were still at Heaslep's.

He reached the main buildings of the big ranch shortly after noon, five leisurely days of riding from San Forenso. Approaching the 'Office,' faces looked out from cook-house, farrier shop, and other doors and windows. Elbert waved and nodded, but there was no flare of welcome, no adequate answer for him—all eyes fixed on what he rode. He had to wait a minute for Frost-face, who appeared from his back room, nodding curtly. He moved at once to the outer door, where his sleety gaze fixed on Mamie at the far end of the rail.

'Your'n?' he asked.

'Yes.'

'In the advertisin' business?'

'No.'

'Been workin' in a movie?'

'No.'

'Show horse?'

'No—'

'Want a job?'

'No. Just thought I'd stop off—possibly see Cal and Slim—and some of the boys.'

'Thought you'd come back to locate. Here's a letter an' telegram. Thoroughbred?'

'Her father was.'

Frost-face moved out to Mamie. The telegram was from Mort Cotton, advising him to wait at Heaslep's for a letter containing a certain newspaper clipping. The letter already at hand, was the one referred to in the telegram, for Elbert drew out a half-page of a Sunday newspaper and a moment later was deep in the latest Sonora doings. Frost-face's jerky tones cut in presently:

'Cal and Slim are out in the northeast range—about fifteen miles. They'll be ridin' farther north to-morrow, but you can get to 'em by sundown. Better drive the truck out, though.'

'The mare isn't tired,' said Elbert.

'Her thorough-breedin' might wilt down.'

'She can do fifteen—'

'Be careful not to let any of the cow-truck out there bite her.'

'I'll watch close.'

'Stop off here for a package of paper napkins and readin' matter to take out to the range—before you start.'

All that afternoon as he rode, Elbert conned the alleged facts of the newspaper story. Monte Vallejo was said to be greatly enlarging the number of his followers, turning away hundreds of peons because they had no horses. This Monte was certainly a cavalry leader first and last, Elbert reflected.... American holdings threatened; gold and silver mines and oil properties of Northern Sonora, unsafe; General Cordano reported to be establishing garrisons near the big mines in an attempt to forestall seizure, but none could tell when Monte Vallejo would strike—

Elbert reached the distant camp at sundown, but full darkness had fallen, before the final thud of ponies on the range grass, and Slim's voice called from outside the circle of firelight.

'... if it ain't Elber-r-rt!'

And big Cal rocked forward, taking him by both shoulders at once—one of those moments when Elbert wouldn't have dared to use his voice.

'What's this I hear about a she race horse you're ridin'?' Slim asked.

Elbert pointed out toward his picket pin, and the two moved toward it. Mamie was led in toward the fire, and examined in all points, her owner being entirely overlooked for the time being.

'Where did you say you come from?' Slim asked severely.

'San Forenso.'

'Any more like that there?'

'I didn't see any.'

'Somebody leavin' the country?'

'She was given to me.'

'Was he dyin'?'

'Yes.'

Cal and Slim glanced at each other.

'Elbert,' said Slim. 'You didn't hurry him off none?'

'No.'

'You see, it *has* been done,' said Cal. 'For a hoss like that, it has been done. I recollect hearin' that old Chester was fought for in his gay young days. Ever hear about that, Slim?'

The other nodded solemnly.

'Ain't back to stay, Elbert?'

'No—'

'Where you goin'?'

The partner's eyes checked off each other again, and finally Cal remarked: 'Looks as if Elbert might need help—'

'He's makin' me restless,' said Slim.

After supper, the three sat down at a small fire a little apart from the main camp. Elbert was watching himself closely, some tension not to be lured into disclosure of any kind. One fact rested lightly on his faculties at this time. The more that men knew about horses, the more Mamie was appreciated. Cal and Slim had opened a newspaper package and divided a big Sunday paper between them.

'Please excuse us, Elbert, while we cool down our passions for news,' said Cal.

A poring silence of many minutes; then from Slim: 'This fellow's crazy.'

'How's that?'

'The fellow writin' this—either crazy, or else there's goin' to be a war less than a hundred miles from here!'

'Who's fightin', Slim?'

'Mexican war—over some oil wells—down San Pasquali way—'

'Any white men?'

'Sure. That's why. This fellow Burton—"Mexicali" Burton—he's American. Struck it rich in oil, but looks to be unpopulyar with a revolutionist, called Vallejo—'

'Just a Sunday newspaper yarn,' said Cal.

'This feller who's writin' says Mister Vallejo could use them oil wells of Burton's to pay off his soldiers and finally take over the government.'

Elbert wasn't breathing right. Another version of the same newspaper story Mort Cotton had sent. He felt as if the truth was being extracted in spite of him; that Cal and Slim had somehow landed into the midst of his private business. Perhaps he shouldn't have come. At the same time, he was powerfully thrilled by some vague prospect, his mind repeating to itself that he had given nothing away so far.

Slim, meanwhile, was reading aloud laboriously about an American oil man, named Burton, who had sent in a call for help to General Juan Cordano, in charge of the Government soldiers in Sonora. This man Burton was said to be standing pat on his property at San Pasquali with a few dozen white men and some Mexican laborers he wasn't at all sure of.

'Every time them newspaper fellers up in Tucson can't think of anything else to write on, they start a Mexican revolution,' Cal said.

'But why couldn't it be?' asked Slim, sitting up straighter, more and more sleepless, his bridle-arm lifted, his right fallen limp as if he were in the saddle. Slim had to wear his belt tight or it would drop down over his hips. One had a feeling that it could be pulled up over his shoulders without loosening a notch. 'Why couldn't it be?' he wanted to know in a louder tone.

'You're breaking in on my rest,' Cal murmured.

Slim straightened out his legs and helped himself to his feet with both hands. Taking a quart cup from his mess-case, he went back to the cook-wagon and returned with it full of hot coffee. 'This ain't no night for rest; this ain't no place for me, Cal. I've been making forty dollars a month so long, anybody'd think I was keepin' up a twenty-year endowment policy—'

The big one bent over to Elbert, whispering: 'I shore hoped he was over them spells. Six months since Slim's been took like this. Sad, ain't it?'

But Elbert saw a reddish flare in Cal's eyes, usually so icy gray and cool. Something queer was taking place in himself at the same time, a wild hope—the last chance on earth. But he couldn't miss that he was forgotten now, the pair more and more involved in each other as the tension grew.

'You'll admit we're dyin' off here,' said Slim.

'Not so loud; hush yourself,' said Cal. 'We ain't got no grudge against Heaslep's. We don't want to start a stampede of hands just as round-up's comin' on.'

'That's so,' Slim muttered.

Elbert suddenly found the eyes of both men boring into his. 'You won't tell 'em anything about this, will you? We ain't got nothin' against old Frost-face,' said Slim.

'I shore would hate to see this outfit left short-handed through any abrupt transformations takin' place between me and Slim,' added Cal.

'I won't say anything,' Elbert declared, but the sound of his own voice was strange and unsteady. A moment later he strolled off into the dark. He didn't trust his face or his feelings which to himself, at least, were conveying meanings louder than words. In a moment or two, Cal's easy tones reached him.

'Elbert!'

He went back.

'Anything eatin' you?'

'No—'

'You ain't figurin'—'

'No, I won't tell Frost-face, or any of the fellows—'

Cal chuckled: 'It ain't that. Slim and me sort of forgot ourselves. Bein' married a long time, it works that way. Can't be you're honin' to perforate the Border like Slim?'

'Wouldn't I slow you up?'

'We thought of that, but concluded we could do with a balancer—'

'I think it would be fine—'

'It'll be a blow to Frost-face, if we do break out. Speak Mexican?'

'I've been studying it lately a little. I had some Latin which helps—'

'Lord, does Latin run in your family, Elbert?'

'I speak Mexican,' Slim reminded, in the tone of one wronged.

Cal squinted at the fire. 'Sure, I forgot. Slim eats her.'

Elbert looked up at the stars. They had suddenly blazed out friendly, and over the cattle came a warm wind and folded him in.

'Excuse me,' Cal added. 'I've got some very close work to do right now— threadin' a needle to tack my war-sack together.'

IX

INITIATION

THEY crossed the Border at Nogales, Cal riding old Chester, Slim on his 'Indian' and Elbert astride.

'Yes, Elbert,' said Cal that first afternoon in Mexico, 'she's shore an indulgence for the eyes.'

A few minutes before sundown they entered the small pueblo of Cienaga. Six hours in the saddle; Elbert was tired, athirst; the early May sunlight had been burning, but except for the occasional oppressive doubt as to his power to carry on without his two friends finding out his real mission, and the fear that his tenderfoot ways might slow up their adventuring, Elbert was possessed by an extraordinary elation; as if part of his lungs that had never known air before, had quietly opened, alive at last.

The moment of fastening the horses at the hitching-rack in the sleepy sandy street, before the little cantina in Cienaga, was memorable from all others in life. There was a dust cloud in the low dobe doorway. Such was the stillness and deep ease in the air, that each grain of dust hung in enticing suspense, a meaning and purpose Elbert was sure of, and needn't try to think out.

'Tequila,' said Slim, as they entered the shadows.

'Same here,' said Cal.

It was like the hold of a ship in a way; the smell of dried orange-peel; a range of barrels with Spanish writing on them, a breath of coolness; shelves of canned and bottled goods, wines and catsup and pickles resting together in dusty composure.

'I will, too,' Elbert said.

The little fat man of the place had been trimming his oil lamp, pouring in coal oil from a large glass jar. He drew out a second piece of glassware from under the counter, slightly smaller, but of similar shape to the first. The contents of the two jars were of identical color.

'Here goes,' said Slim, and the three small glasses were raised.

For a second Elbert thought he had been shot in the neck. Out of the pandemonium of his faculties then formed the suspicion that either they burned tequila in the lamps, or else that was the Mexican name for kerosene.

'The first one always hits me where I ain't lookin',' Cal remarked. 'Suppose we go through the formalities of three more.'

Elbert braced to do it again. He felt himself standing very straight, only there was a curious illusion that his spine extended clear through to the top of his head. The reverberations of the second shot having died away, Elbert was conscious of a faint aroma, as if all the dried fruits and tubers and woodwork had blent in enticing fragrance. A horse nickered from afar down the street and their three ponies at the hitching-rail raised their heads—Mamie's instant answer being ramified by Chester's dignified head-tones, and a shrill broken pipe from the 'Indian.' A kind of union and interplay in all things—glint of drift and daring in Cal Monroid's eyes. The little fat man was shaking his match box. It really wouldn't do for the lamp to be lighted just yet. Elbert spoke up:

'We might risk one more,' he said with slow care.

Now Cal and Slim took his invitation in a queer way. They pawed each other and kept saying: 'I told you so.' Could they mean they weren't regretting they had let him come?

'I like it here,' said Slim.

'I feel like stayin',' said Cal. 'I could eat some of these here dried herrin' and pickles standin' up, but I suggests we saunter to a table somewhere and feed on somethin' firm. I could stay all night—'

Elbert, standing very straight, turned away to the doorway that last moment before the lamp was lighted, and there he beheld his Crimson Foam—the whole West over the horses' heads, shot with Indian red. It was worth the beginning at Heaslep's, the struggle with Fortitude, the leather-store and even the years of Eastern schooling. Only he mustn't fall to telling how joyous he was. Meanwhile Slim and the little fat man were having words. The former turned to Cal with his wronged look:

'What you goin' to do with a fellow like this? He keeps hornin' in with English. Says I called him a horse. Says I mean caballero, not caballo. Wants to know if we'll have our chickens boiled or fried.'

'Quickest for me,' said Cal. 'Only tell him I ain't broke off with beans.'

After supper, Cal suggested that they go out to the corral to see if the horses were making out as well as they were. Elbert sat back against a stone. The straw smelled dry and clean; the sky was close and velvety; the three horses were grinding sun-parched corn, a soothing sound; everything expansive and exactly right, only a persistent tendency to be reminiscent, which Elbert checked. Finally at his right, a chuckle from Cal:

'Slim—'

'Yep?'

'For a tenderfoot, I'm sayin' our young friend Elbert holds his fire-water aloft some successful, don't you think?'

Slim allowed that, and Elbert's face turned away to the dark, so his exultation might not be seen. He felt on the eve of a mysterious graduation ceremony....

Toward mid-afternoon two days later they entered the pueblo of Nacimiento, and two thin dogs skulked across the road ahead of their horses. An old man, beyond human speech, was sitting in the sun against a wall, and a little farther on, another. That seemed the end of life, as they paused before a fonda marked 'El Cajon.' The sandy road at this point was beaten with many pony tracks.

'Looks as if a troop of cavalry had halted here,' Slim said in a hushed tone.

A moment of rich promise to Elbert, except that he wished he didn't feel so played out. They entered the deserted wine-room. Slim drew a finger over the bar-board and left his mark in the dust. A scared lame boy finally came out from the shadows behind. No mistake about his gestures; they were urged to move on.

'What do you think we're up against?' Cal inquired. 'Yellow fever or just war?'

'Can't say,' said Slim, 'only far from home—far from home.'

'We might keep on going to Burton's oil wells at San Pasquali. Can't be more than eighteen miles from here, but it would take the edge off the horses; also what little nape of Elbert's, as ain't wore off already.'

'Oh, I'm all right,' Elbert hastened to say, 'whatever you think best.'

At the end of town they heard a phonograph, the twisty piping tones of 'El Chocolo.' In a doorway presently appeared a barefooted old woman with a broom in one hand and a pair of castanets in the other. Slim uncorked his Spanish. It sounded to Elbert as if he were asking for rooms with bath. The Senora's mouth opened, but no sound came. She raised one foot and clucked the castanets, finally coördinating:

'No sabe, Señor.'

Slim repeated.

The other foot vanished; the castanets vibrated and a single word shot forth: 'Baños,' was the nature of it, the Señora pointing to a tin wash-tub under the eaves. At this point Elbert had to attend to Mamie, who wasn't taking to the Señora and her castanets. Her feet were planted firmly against advance to the hitching-rack, and a long, tremulous wheeze poured out of her nostrils, signifying distrust, alarm.

'I'll love up the Señora,' said Slim, confidently. He dismounted and bowed low. The Mexican woman couldn't resist and turned into the doorway, bidding them follow. Mamie now relaxed, and Elbert was the last to enter a flowered patio, where the Señora brought pans of water for them to wash, and then began stirring in the ashes of the ancient fireplace.

'I'm takin' on hope,' Cal breathed. 'She's fixin' to boil something, if it's only grool.'

'Frijoles,' lightly called Slim. 'Also, huevos, Señora, also tortillas tom bien.'

Her back was toward them, her face still bent over the fireplace, but her hand shot up, registering the orders on the castanets.

At this instant something began to be wrong in the air. A far-off sound took the heart out of Elbert; hatefully familiar, it was, spoiling at once all the mysterious warnings of deserted Nacimiento—the chug-chug of an earth-eater, high-powered, and coming fast.

A small, square, vined window in the patio faced the road. Elbert moved to it, Cal and Slim following. The three heads looked out, a hush fallen upon them. A cherry-colored sedan, dust of Mexico unable to cover its incredible modernity, halted before the Señora's door, and three queer boyish figures hopped out.

X

'WATER IS FOR HORSES'

'THEY'RE white,' whispered Slim. 'They're play-actors.'

Then from Cal: 'What kind of little boys would you say them were, Elbert?'

'I wouldn't. They're girls in hikin' clothes. Don't you see their vanities?'

'Short hair and short pants, Elbert—where do you look for them points you speak of—oh, you mean them little satchels?'

Mexico had petered out; hope dead.

'You go in first, Elbert. I never coped with nothin' like them,' Cal murmured.

They followed the Señora into the front room. A chunky, black-haired girl, who had sat in the driver's seat of the sedan, was letting it be known that she and her two friends had stopped for refreshments, on their way to San Pasquali. Her voice was resonant, and she tried to make volume do, being without Spanish.

The Señora held up her empty hand; her mouth opened, no sound. Slim hurried back to the fireplace to fetch her clappers.

The black-haired one stamped her foot. She was used to getting what she wanted. 'Oh, can't you see, we're hungry, thirsty—something to eat and drink?'

She had muscle, and big blue eyes.

'Put your hand on your belt. Miss,' Cal called. 'Make signs of bein' caved in.'

'Hush up, Cal. That ain't no language to use,' said Slim, stepping up from the side. 'Allow me to interperate for you, lady.'

'Thanks, if you please.'

At this point Elbert's hand touched a hand at his left. He turned and said 'Excuse me,' in severe tones. A swift shy smile met his eyes—the face of one unmistakably frightened, but handling it—a girl who could cry engagingly, but only after everything was over. Her tones had a curious way of not disturbing the stillness.

'I think we made a mistake in coming—an awful mistake,' she laughed. 'I told Florabel we ought to turn round and go back, but she wouldn't hear to it—'

Elbert turned to Florabel whose blue eyes were flashing up to Cal's. 'I'm Miss Burton, and I'm going to San Pasquali to surprise Papa!'

'Won't you, though!' enthused Cal.

The third of the girls was smaller, younger—a whitish, wide-eyed face, hovering above a large and high-colored necktie. Slim had taken over this little one, but she was slow to soothe, her eyes getting wider, the white of her skin fading into colorless fear. Meanwhile, in shy tones, Elbert was hearing the story of their coming from the girl at his left.

'We're from Miss Van Whipple's Finishing School in Tucson. It's spring vacation now, and we were sight-seeing in Nogales this morning, when Florabel got the idea to rush down here and see her father. It was only seventy miles, she said, and wouldn't take more than three hours, and then we'd be safe. I'm afraid we've made a terrible mistake—'

'I'm afraid you have,' said Elbert. He was used to a houseful of sisters and he carried no heartstrings whatsoever for passing winds to flap.

Her name was Mary Gertling. Her short hair was neither black nor blonde, but there was a roll to it, down over her temples, that Elbert remembered as a sort of aim of all his sisters' girl friends before he left. He forgot what Mary was saying for a minute, studying the creamy light through her skin. It made him remember the thin bowl of alabaster on the ceiling of the dining-room at home. She didn't seem to mind his severe ways. She just couldn't seem to believe it of him. He recalled the ominous signs which attended their riding into Nacimiento, the many pony tracks.

'If I were you, I'd ask Miss Burton to turn around now and go back,' he said.

'But Florabel never would. She never turns back—in anything. She says her father is less than twenty miles from here.'

She talked up to him so trustingly. The little fawnskin coat covering her shoulders had that texture which draws the hand to touch. Her ways were swift and still; but Elbert had lost his revolution and his heart held hard as flint.

'Come on, Mary!' called Miss Florabel.

The three girls followed the Señora into the patio. Elbert stood in deep thought a moment, before he realized that Cal and Slim had closed in upon him.

'Our little Elbert ain't no hosstipath,' said Slim. 'I've seen smoother hands all around with hosses, but for women and motor trucks he's faster than a coiled whip—'

'Faster than the human eye,' said Cal.

'They belong to the Van Whipple Finishin' School up in Tucson,' Elbert said thoughtfully.

'So we draws.'

'It's vacation. They were sight-seeing in Nogales. They ought to be sent back—'

'We heard you tell her!'

'It's all this Burton girl's fault.'

'Slim,' said Cal, unheeding, 'you and me ain't got no sway with this finishin' school, if Elbert ain't.'

'We've got to have some sway,' said Slim, 'or it's goin' to be the plumb finish.'

'What do you think our duty is?' Elbert asked absently.

'Our duty, I'd say, by these finishers,' Slim whispered with considerable weight, 'our duty is to stay with 'em whether they like it or not, and I'm meanin' to do just that, only—' He pointed to an empty place in the room where the littlest of the girls had stood, 'Only, every time I takes a step to her, this little one with the rainbow necktie and the ruffle on her uniform, she looks as if she's goin' to stagnate down an' die. I shore expects a bleat out of her, my next step, and all the time I see Elbert out of the corner of my eye, gettin' closer and closer and talkin' lower and faster—'

'Must be some perfume he has on,' said Cal.

'I didn't take it she was particular afraid of my advance,' modified Slim, 'just generally hos-tile. I sure drew the outlaw, though.'

'Perhaps,' suggested Cal, 'if we turn over little Rainbow to Elbert, we could manage the other two.'

'That is as nature fixes it, Cal. We'd have some trouble right now, tearin' that little Mary female away from Elbert, the inroads he's made. But no use standin' here. I'm goin' to get a pair of knives and whetstone out of my war bags an' freshen up for supper.'

'You're not meanin' to shave, Slim?'

'That's the presumption.'

Elbert rustled hay from the shed and carried it out to the hitching-rack, the Señora's house being suspiciously short-handed. Half way between the corral and the kitchen door, he sat down, and moodily watched the Señora getting supper. She did her work on the run, back and forth in the old stone kitchen, castanets off. Her bare feet seemed to roll up under her as she sped, one at a time reappearing to give the stone floor a shove. It was like a double-action paddlewheel. Curious sizzlings reached his ears from the open fire, also fascinating scents. He was sure sliced onions were curling and browning on the pan.

Supper was set for six. Elbert found Mary Gertling seated at his left. He rose from the table to get a glass of water, but the Señora prevented, thrusting red wine in his hands.

'Vino tinto! Vino tinto!' she exclaimed.

'I'm s'prised, Elbert,' Slim corrected. 'Didn't you know water is for the horses?'

'Isn't everything wonderful?' whispered Mary Gertling.

'Do you think so?' Elbert inquired.

'Dulzura!' flamed Slim; then Cal's easy voice as he monopolized the attention of Florabel Burton: 'So your father hasn't written to you none, Miss, that there's a mixture of politics going on about his oil wells?'

'Oh, yes. Papa always allows for that. He says it wouldn't be Mexico—if there wasn't some trouble in the air.'

'No special trouble lately—things comin' to a head?'

'Oh, let's go back!' trembled the voice from behind the big necktie.

'Just take it easy, lady,' in Slim's gentlest corral tones.

'Things are always coming to a head down here,' said Miss Burton.

'I know,' said Cal, 'I can understand just how you feel. But we're concerned, especially Elbert here. If you knew that boy as well as I do, you'd seen by his face that he's sick with concern right now.'

'Oh, Florabel!' said Mary Gertling. 'Can't we ask them to go with us? I'll breathe so much easier.'

'Oh, let's!' faintly from the little one, whom they called Imogen.

'Why, we'll be down there in an hour, before it's really dark!' Florabel objected, but finally gave way.

XI

GAS AND GUNS

ELBERT smelled gas, as he rode behind the sedan. It had always been so; gas belonged to the deep fatigue of his bones. One of the keenest minutes he had ever lived was that in which they had leaned down toward the wide tangle of tracks in front of the fonda marked El Cajon—all able-bodied men gone from Nacimiento, and big doings promised farther on. And then, a matter of mere minutes afterward, his old enemy had come roaring down the dirt road. Girls—everything spoiled—Cal and Slim all changed around.

The sedan was just rolling forward, but it kept the ponies at a lope. It seemed hours; the sliver of a moon had sunk out of the sky. Florabel's resonant voice reached him from the car. No secret now why 'Mexicali' Burton dared to stand off Northern Sonora for his oil wells—the father of this girl would be like that. Cal loomed in the dark, having waited for Mamie to come up.

'Your lady-friend's got her mind made up to sit a horse for a ways, Elbert. Slim's Indian ain't that kind of a horse, and your Mamie's a filly yet. I figure she'd better try old Chester, but you sort of ride close and keep him consoled and her camped in the right place.'

'How about you, Cal?'

'Nothin' else will do, but I'm to test my morals in the little red buggie.'

The transfer was made. Elbert rode on through the thick May dark with Mary Gertling at his left.

'I've been on a horse before,' she said.

No answer.

'I'm afraid you think I'm being a trouble.'

Still Elbert's lips were locked. He couldn't see her clearly, but her hands certainly were not in sight. Nobody with any sense of a horse would leave her hands in her lap.

'Oh, I'm afraid you don't like to have me here!' reached him in the stillness.

'Sure. Pick up your reins. We're falling back—'

'But he bumps so—'

'They don't make horses any smoother than he is. Want to get back in the car?'

'No-o.'

'You're doing all right.' He had lied in spite of himself, and this didn't make him feel any better. Old Chester, tired as he was, couldn't be expected to keep his feet trim, with no hand of authority communicating with the bit. Heat increased under Elbert's collar. A heave in the road and his left hand shot out before he thought. It was clutched. Warm, small, firm. The two horses pulled apart a little, but the hand didn't let go. He was afraid of yanking her out of the saddle.

'I'm so sorry to make you cross. I think it was awful for Florabel to think of coming—oh—I'm falling!'

The hand slid out of his. He hurriedly dismounted. Mary was hanging sideways, both hands on the pommel. Elbert knew the abused look of Chester's head, hanging low in the dark. He pushed her back up in the saddle.

'Need any help?' Slim sang back from in front.

'No!'

'Why, Elbert, I never heard such tones as them, spoke from you before—'

'Oh, please don't be cross!' in a whisper from his side. 'I don't know what I'd ever have done—'

'Oh, that's all right.' The miles were the longest in his experience. During the last twenty minutes the horses had trudged up hill, the motor making noisy business of the grade. Then the ridge and lights below, San Pasquali, doubtless. Elbert fancied he smelled the oil wells. He would never get away from gasoline.

'Hadn't you better get into the car?' he remarked to Mary Gertling.

Cal was back on old Chester. The sedan had just started down-grade, when Elbert saw three red perforations in the dark ahead. The fraction of a second later, three separate concussions shocked his ears—not gas explosions, guns! There was one scream—from the little one—and Cal's yell directed toward the car, as he spurred forward. 'Better turn back, Miss—they may have the town surrounded!'

Slim's Indian and Mamie had settled down after Chester. Shouts of Mexicans sounded beyond the car, just as Elbert's mare came to abrupt stop. The sedan had halted, too, but the lights still pointed straight ahead. Florabel wasn't making the turn; she was either shocked helpless, or her engine stalled. In the wide fling of the head-lights, Elbert saw armed Mexicans standing across the road. Then they started this way—six or seven figures running toward them, hands upraised, rifles held aloft For once Cal's voice lost its drawl.

'Get in the car, Kid! Let your horse go!'

Elbert's leg lifted out of the stirrup—one of the hardest things he was ever called to do, but that very second the lights of the sedan went out. There was one clear call from Mary Gertling, deadened by a blasting roar from the sedan's exhaust at the very knees of his mount. Too much for Mamie. She went straight up and tried to keep going, Elbert at the very top, arms around her frantic throat at the narrowest—as the darkened sedan gouged forward like a speed-boat. Cal's voice reached him:

'... that Burton girl—she's shootin' the lines! Come on, Slim, it means us, too! Come on, Kid!'

Shots in the air—shots from ahead and at the sides.

He felt Mamie tottering still on her hind feet; then a jerk as if some one had given her a cut with a whip, and over she went backward. He pushed her neck from him and fell back, and knew no more, until Cal's low tones, as he was being lifted.

'It's all right. Kid. Chester's good for both of us.'

For a time, in spite of that, he thought he still had Mamie round the neck, but it was Cal's ample chest—Slim's Indian in an easy gallop alongside.

'Where's the sedan?' he finally mumbled.

'Lord, Kid, she's surprised papa by this time!'

- 59 -

XII

FLASHLIGHT AND FAWNSKIN

ELBERT kept shaking his head; no bones broken there or elsewhere, but seemingly no end to the phases of his coming-to. It dawned on him there had been a blank from the time Mamie went over backwards, until he found himself here on Chester with Cal. He regretted missing some part in there—going through the Mexican lines.

'Where's Mamie?' he demanded, jerking erect.

'Came through all right. Slim's got her safe.'

Now Elbert gradually made out that they were in 'Mexicali' Burton's oil town. They had been halted—first a voice in Mexican, then American, Cal answering quietly. He saw the sedan, and heard from aside in the dark, Mamie's long-drawn wheeze, the same protest as when she had refused advance to the hitching-rail before the Señora's house in Nacimiento. There was one cabin door from which light streamed, and in the aperture a blocky, bareheaded man appeared, legs planted wide apart, the air suddenly burned by withering profanities.

'... bringin' three young women through Vallejo's lines!... Sap-heads, you fellows. It's running out of your ears!'

'I'm not takin' no free talk from no oil man,' growled Slim.

Cal mildly broke in. 'Now as to that, Mister—'

'Can't you see we've got a war on?' the blocky one in the doorway yelled. 'Can't you see they're twenty to one, tryin' to get our oil wells?' His face had turned sidewise; light fell upon the uncovered, close-cropped head— massive jaw, thin lips and startlingly familiar blue eyes. Around that roaring neck from behind, a pair of white arms were flung at this instant, 'Mexicali's' fury shut off:

'But Papa! I keep telling you it was all my fault!'

Florabel had the floor, but another figure had moved into the light behind her. 'You see, Mr. Burton, when we three wouldn't turn back, they rode along with us, to protect us.' That was Mary Gertling. So they had all reached the cabin.

Elbert still felt confused. Slim's voice broke in now, stern with dignity. 'Seein' as there's no further need for us to be engaged in protectin'—otherwise we might ride on—'

Another rip. '... ride on what? Ride on where? Don't you see we're surrounded?'

'Papa!'

'Mexicali' slowed down to bellow orders to his men, both Mexicans and Americans hurrying in and out. He rang bells in both languages. Meanwhile Cal and Slim had entered the lamp-lit quarters, and Elbert followed, meeting the eyes of Mary Gertling. Still those eyes hadn't broken into tears; still that inexplicable stillness around her—the same faint trace of a smile, as in the first moment in Nacimiento.

Now 'Mexicali' Burton and Cal Monroid were facing each other, like two chiefs—one instantaneous look. All they had seemed to need was this one look in the lamplight. Each knew a man. It was a moment of romantic fulfillment to Elbert. His mind had suddenly renewed its grasp on the fact that Bart Leadley might be a part of Vallejo's lines now closing about; yet at the same time he could not miss the way the fighting face of 'Mexicali' Burton had suddenly softened and turned in appeal to Cal.

'It was bad enough before,' he was saying, slowly. 'Vallejo's got numbers. I trust my white men, but you never can trust the Mexicans. Cordano himself may double-cross me. Can't tell when he'll get some troops here. It was bad enough before, but what can a man do with three girls—?'

A whimsical smile was on Cal's lips, which formed to answer, but the words were never spoken.

That was the instant the gods of North America undertook to get a flash-light photograph of the lower end—stupefying flash and crash—blinding glare, heaving darkness, falling timbers, the scream of one horse.

Elbert was on his knees, eyes and nostrils choked with dust. He thought of Mamie outside; then certain new business and nothing else occupied his brain. In that unbelievable glare, he had seen the face of Mary Gertling. The light hadn't shone upon her face, it had flowed into it, through it. He had seen the secret of her stillness, and though he couldn't recall the nature of it now, he was perfectly aware that an explosion like that might breed another and he must somehow get to her, before it happened again.

He was calling. She called back just once. He was groping for her now. His hand touched objects, but they had nothing to do with what he groped for. His ears were filled with voices, but he was really listening only for one. His fingers touched the little fawnskin jacket, and beneath his face as he knelt, there was the queerest low sob; one arm came up and held him, and the words:

'You shouldn't have been quite so long—'

At his side was the distracting rattle of a match box, the strike of the stick. A face appeared—'Mexicali' Burton—all below the eyes, a gleaming black of blood.

'Florabel!'

'Papa!'

'You and the other two—get into the sedan—before they explode the second powder house. One of my own natives probably. Get into—get into the sedan—' subdued, sincere, not an extra syllable. Father and daughter—they had found each other. Cal and Slim had found each other. Elbert bent. 'I didn't mean to be so long—' he said.

The one arm tightened around him. Another match was struck. Florabel screamed at the sight of her father's face. 'Mexicali' drew the hollow of his sleeve down over it. 'Shut up, Flo',' he said in the same subdued way. 'Just a scratch. Pile into the sedan—'

'I can't move.'

'You must—who's this lyin' across your lap?'

'That's Imogen. She's fainted. She did it before.'

'I'll put her into the sedan. Come on—'

'I can't—'

'I'll lift you in.'

'I can't drive—' The sentences shot back and forth; even Cal Monroid spoke: 'Speakin' of drivin'—that's the Kid's job—' all while the second match burned.

'Sure, Elbert'll drive,' from Slim.

Elbert bent again. 'We've got to go to the sedan.'

'Yes—' from under his lips, but she did not stir.

'Come on. Won't you help me?'

'Oh, yes—'

'Can you walk?'

'Yes.'

'Come then—they're putting Imogen in.'

'But you—'

'I'm going with you—'

'Oh!'

He felt the queer uncertainty of her body, as she gained her feet, yet she seemed trying to help him. Yes, she had promised to help; her one hand was actually trying to lift him, at the same time holding on.

Florabel and Imogen were in the back of the car. He couldn't see if they were rightly in the seats. Elbert took the wheel, and drew Mary Gertling in after him. Her hand didn't feel right. Another hand was now thrust in through the door after Mary was seated—'Mexicali's'—wet, hot, hairy.

'You've got to get there, young fellow!'

'Yes, sir.'

'Clear through to Nogales.'

'Yes, sir.'

'I'll vouch for Elbert,' came from Cal, who seemed standing just behind Burton.

'But how about Mamie?'

'Slim and me'll take care of her.'

'I ain't gone over her, but she's on her feet.' This last was from Slim. 'We'll keep her for you.'

'You can't take the road you came by—not for a ways.' 'Mexicali' went on, thickly. 'Keep goin' toward the derricks. Follow the wheel-tracks; they'll work you back to the main road later. Use your lamps—when you have to—'

'Papa—'

'Don't bother me!' The voice was thick, as if 'Mexicali's' throat was filling with blood. 'We're stayin' here, but these oil wells aren't a hell of a lot, compared to the baggage you're carryin', young fellow. Clear through to Nogales, do you hear?'

'He'll get through, Mister,' said Cal, and then the same voice trailed, 'So long, Kid.'

XIII

VALLEJO'S LINES

ELBERT'S mind didn't steady down at once to the wheel. A moaning kept up from behind. That was Imogen. Part of him, too, seemed listening for Florabel's voice; he had vaguely counted on her undertaking to drive from the back seat, as his sisters used to, but not a word.... Gasoline.... Girls.... 'Thirty years late.'... Tequila—coal-oil—vino tinto.... 'Water is for horses.'... Mamie.... Thus his mind kept churning, as if to get a certain harrowing review out of the way, before he took up the matter at hand. Certainly matters at hand—the wheel, the girl at his side. He expected her hand to rise out of the dark and tangle him further, but it didn't come. Queer to have her on his right. She had been on his left always before.

He was following the wheel-tracks among the derricks, using his lights when he had to. Perhaps he was getting close to the second powder house; anyway, he was doing what he was told.... He wasn't exactly right; he had to stop to think that he wasn't back in old Fortitude's stiff-backed seat. A deep hurt about leaving Mamie behind and not being exactly true to his secret quest, preyed upon him; also the possibility that Bart Leadley was within a mile of him at this moment, working with Vallejo to get Burton's oil. A voice shouted from ahead—Mexican—part of Vallejo's cordon. Now Bart or not, he had to get down to business. He had baggage. He had to get through.

All was black before his eyes. He was holding the sedan to a mental picture of the dirt road, impressed upon his memory an instant ago when he turned on the lights, but the black scaffoldings of the derricks wove crazily before his eyes; the chance of a smash taking his breath. He felt the wheel jerk as it left the tire-grooves. A row of rifle flashes showed ahead; glass splintered around them.

'Get down—way down,' he gasped.

He pressed the throttle, holding the wheel toward the guns; the engine roared underfoot. The firing was from behind now, but he kept going into the blackness until he couldn't risk another second; the sense of leaping off into an abyss of darkness was so keen.

Lights showed the wheel-tracks; still the derricks on either hand. Not a sound or a touch from his side. More rifles cracked ahead. It had to be done again.

'Get down, way down!' he called. Again the car shot forward through the flashes. This time hands touched the outside; bumps of metal, more splintered glass. The wheel jerked out of his hand; the sedan ditched, but didn't overturn. In a flash of one rifle, he saw a second figure—mouth open, pistol raised. He seemed to look right into that open mouth and belching muzzle. The fenders on the same side screeched against stone.

He wasn't right. He had to throw his body forward on the wheel to hold it, as he turned on the lights—only the right hand working. He was back in the wheel-tracks, but the car kept fighting away from him—a flat tire. He felt an absurd need to explain. 'It was that left front tire that threw me—' but she wasn't listening. His foot sank upon the throttle.

Now Elbert was badly mixed about that left front tire and his own left side—both flat. He had to hurry now while his right arm lasted. 'I'll vouch for Elbert.... He'll get through, Mister.... So long, Kid.' But all the time he was getting farther and farther from Mamie—from Bart!

The wheel-tracks had circled back to the main road. His right foot steadied down. He had to hold the wheel with all his strength to make up for the retard on the left.... Not a touch or a sound from his side. Thirst was stealing into him like the cold. Maybe she was thirsty.... Maybe they wouldn't know which was which—tequila, coal oil.... 'I've been on a horse before.... He bumps so.'... 'Thirty years late.'... He had lights; he held to the highway, his foot pressed to the floor.... She wasn't helping—not a touch, or did she mean to help by keeping still?

———————————

Vaguely Elbert heard low words like this:

'He doesn't relax. He keeps listening for a voice. The rest of the time he seems to think he's driving something—a horse or a car. It's not always clear. If he could only stop driving himself, every time he comes to, and get some rest'—a strange woman's voice.

'Put him to sleep again,' a man replied from the far side of the room. 'I'll answer his father's telegram, but nobody could satisfy these newspaper men, and have time for anything else.'

Of course, they didn't understand. He had to get through. He had to keep on, while his right arm lasted—clear through to Nogales. And even if he did, it wouldn't mean that he was making good to what he set out for. He had passed up the main chance, falling for another. There was a pricking in his right arm now, but no sound from that side, not a word—everything muffled and getting farther away ... until Cal's easy tones really began to set him straight:

'Take it easy, Kid. You got 'em here—right here in Nogales! You brought 'em through—days ago. Listen, Kid, you don't need to drive no more!' That voice always straightened things out.

'But Mamie—' he finally broke out.

'She's waitin' for you. We brought her up—fine—'

Elbert felt himself moving softly after that, into an altogether different zone of sleep. 'But where?' He locked his lips. He mustn't ask anything more.

Cal came again, and finally with Slim, but it was a dreary time before they let him ask questions. Mamie was right here in Nogales. 'Mexicali' Burton's party had held out until morning at San Pasquali, when General Cordano had come, driving Vallejo away.

'Did he lose any men?' Elbert mumbled.

'Who?'

'Vall—I mean Cordano—or Mr. Burton?'

'Some,' said Slim, suspicious of delirium again.

... Another time, and they were telling him everything but what he wanted especially to know. Yes, Mexicali with a crushed jaw had kept on his pins all through that night of the explosion, until relief came. 'He's here in Nogales right now—jaw in a sling,' added Cal.

Elbert craftily inquired about Florabel.

'She got broke somewhere—I didn't hear where,' said Slim.

'Not so she ain't goin' to recover,' finished Cal.

Elbert's lips forced him to say, 'And little Rainbow?'

'Not a scratch,' said Slim. 'She just fainted and wasn't there to get hurt—when that explosure took place.'

Elbert was silent. Cal's voice took up the story: 'As for that little Mary-woman, I'm holdin' a letter for you she left before her parents took her up to Tucson.'

It was like splintered glass, the way Slim broke in: 'We'd better go, Cal. Elbert ain't lookin' as well as he should.'

Cal arose: 'She got all right before she left, except for one broken arm.'

Several seconds ticked, before the question: 'Which arm?'

'Now it was the left arm, as I recall.'

'Oh, I see, she couldn't—' Elbert halted with a jerk. It seemed they never would go.

XIV

A LETTER

THEY had put out the lights. Even the night-light at the far end of the hall was turned low, but sentences wrote themselves out on the ceiling; a pause, then a sentence; a pause, then another.

'... *Could it have been the wine she gave us at supper—the barefooted old woman? I was so very thirsty!... I can't understand. I can't believe, yet I distinctly remember insisting that I ride that horse.... I was so horribly frightened—except when I was near you.... I couldn't help seeing how the others turned to you.... Won't you please believe I never acted like that before?... It was because you were so firm—that I could breathe better where you were.... And in the car—it was like hanging on a cross, wasn't it?... Oh, won't you get word to me that you forgive?*'

Such a stillness around each sentence.

XV

TUCSON

HE was sitting up when Cal and Slim came again. That was the day of the telegram that his father was leaving the East and would be in Tucson in three days more. Also there were more Tucson and Border papers with a lot extra to say about Vallejo's attack on the San Pasquali oil wells; of the rescue of the American party by Mexican government troops; but especially of the motor drive of one white man through the rebel's lines—seventy miles north, clear through to Nogales—how the car had been found at dawn at the edge of town, the driver close to death from a gunshot wound in his left side, two American girls unconscious in the car, and another unhurt, but too scared to talk.

'Not a drop of gas in the tank or you'd have rammed right into the Border, Elbert,' Cal said.

'You sure stepped on the oats,' said Slim.

'We didn't get to stay in Mexico,' Elbert complained after a time. 'We had to come right back.'

Cal and Slim looked at each other, faces long and grave.

'He didn't get to stay,' said Cal.

'Only one horse went over back with him,' said Slim. 'Only one powder magazine blew up. Only hit by one forty-five—'

'Had to come right back,' said Cal.

'I thought I'd get to ride,' said Elbert, 'but I had to drive that car—'

Cal inquired after a moment: 'Do you reckon we might take Elbert along again sometime?'

'I ain't a well man. I ain't ready to state as to that right now',' said Slim. 'I need to be babied along at Heaslep's, where they ain't rough, and talk gentle—'

'He wants to hear about old hoof-and-mouth,' Cal suggested.

'They're going to let me out of here to-morrow,' said Elbert. 'I'll be goin' up to Tucson—to meet my father.'

Elbert was clear of the hospital before he began to see things straight. In fact, he was standing with Mamie in her box stall the next day in the livery stable at Nogales, on the American side, when some perfectly useless frictions and pressures fell away. In the first place, here was Mamie safe and sound, and the future opened with a new chance to begin over again at the bottom. Had he lost the mare, there could have been no real beginning over, at the bottom or anywhere else. Secondly, he hadn't divulged his secret, even in delirium. Certain time had been lost, the fault his in deciding to stop at Heaslep's for a friendly call on the way from San Forenso to the Border.

Beyond doubt he must travel alone from now on. He was breathing easier. A bit weak on his legs—too long in bed—but ready to begin again. Queer, how it all cleared up for him standing with Mamie like this. 'Stand around and talk to her,' Bob Leadley had said. 'She likes to be consulted on family affairs. It won't do you no harm. She's one more listening mare.'

'I'll just leave you right here, Mamie,' he whispered, 'while I go up to Tucson for a day or two. These people seem to be treating you right—and it's handy to the Border. Take it easy till I come back, because we'll be losing ourselves in work after that.'

... A queer, embarrassed half-embrace, neither knowing just what to do or say, and a swift look into his father's eyes after several months—really the first exchange that had the beginnings of understanding in it. Elbert finally grasped what a son is so slow to find out—that his father was not merely a parent, but a separate human being, with his own struggles, silences, dilemmas, like the rest of the world. It was Elbert's first understanding of his own house, and the man of it, from the attitude of an outsider. Another moment of a fresh beginning in life, he realized. Meanwhile sentences like this were passing:

'Got yourself pretty badly shot up?'

'It was a bad jumble for a minute—'

'But you saw them through—'

'I had to. I don't even remember, most of it.'

'Come on, let's go in to dinner.... No, Nancy isn't married yet, but the house feels as if news might break out any day—likely by the time I—we—get back—'

The last was nothing like a foregone conclusion, but phrased tentatively, with questioning look.

'No, I won't be going back just yet,' Elbert said.

He felt the silence; also suddenly he felt his father's side as well as his own. A man accustomed to a houseful of daughters might really want to have his only son standing beside him very much. It was an entirely new angle.

'Haven't got enough?'

'Not quite through—'

'Going back to Heaslep's?'

'Oh, no—'

No resistance from his father. Elbert hardly knew how to handle this new man-to-man acquiescence—no tampering. He had braced himself, but no strength was required; and now for a moment he was unnerved by friendliness. Was his father changed, because of things the newspapers said about his drive to Nogales? A whole lot of stuff had been written which no fellow could pay any attention to, about himself. Elbert began to feel an almost irresistible impulse to tell the whole story to his father.

'Not going back to San Pasquali?' the latter asked.

'No.'

'I was hoping you didn't mean to tie up with this man, Burton—'

'Oh, no.'

'And those friends of yours—those cowhands—'

'I'm planning to be alone for a while.'

Elbert's answers were automatic. A fight was still on in him, not to divulge about Bob Leadley and the gold mine. It seemed almost that his father had the right to know—but Elbert kept his mouth shut.

Toward the end of dinner the elder man said with a laugh: 'You'll be needing some money—'

'No, I'm all fixed, thanks.'

Elbert couldn't follow his father's reaction to that. Mr. Sartwell said nothing, but seemed both glad and sorry at the same time. After that he spoke with even a little more care, not to impose his will. It was like two men talking in a club, about anything in the world, except what each meant to the other.

Elbert was waiting in the reception room of the Finishing School. It was the summer season and only a few of the girls were staying over—those whose families did not live in Tucson, possibly. The place was shaded and flowery; blossoms on all the tables, and one great basket, shaped like a French hat of an old day, on the piano, filled with young pink roses. He heard laughter and whispering in the hallway. It wasn't exactly clear to him what he must say or do. He felt his wound right now, a sort of general breakdown. The door he was looking toward—the direction the voices came from—didn't open. Her step sounded from behind. He saw her first among the vines at the window, facing the porch. Her lips moved, her hand lifted, the door opened, but everything was stiller than one could imagine.

'I would have known you—'

'Of course—'

'It's probably because I saw you before—I mean before dark that night—'

He felt a vague surprise in himself that he caught the drift so readily. 'At the barefooted woman's—' he finished.

'Yes—'

'It was different, after supper that night,' she went on, 'but I'm glad I would have known you, as you are to-day. Reading the papers was so confusing.'

'They never know when to stop.'

'They didn't tell it nearly all, either—'

'What do you mean?'

'Oh, I wouldn't have known it was the same story by reading it in the papers.'

'I see—'

She was changed—less glitter somehow, as if her light came from deeper in, a light more delicate. She had on a creamy dress, no folds in it, but not tight anywhere. This meeting wasn't like the first time in the Señora's house; nor yet, was it like the sense of her which had come in the hospital, from so many hours of pondering over the separate sentences of her letter. Suddenly he knew he must never tie himself to any particular moment when with her, because she wasn't going to be the same the next time. Tying to one meeting would keep him from catching on to all that the next held in store. His mind clung for a moment, however, to the memory of the alabaster bowl at home, while she was still going on about the newspapers.

'They didn't see you. They didn't know what we did—what we tried to do. They sort of laughed at us, and talked of your great bravery, but there was something no one saw—'

She was standing at his left—a hush between the sentences. '... They didn't know that somebody was helping us—'

'What do you mean?'

'I mean it wasn't just your strength. Why, you were like one dead; and yet you still drove. It was only when we were safe that your hand relaxed—'

'A case of knowing I had to, wasn't it?'

'More than that. That helped, of course, but there was something more—'

He said: 'I didn't know much of what was happening at the time—that is, to remember, but I had a feeling you were helping—'

'Did you know that?'

'Yes.'

'Really, did you know that?'

'I had the feeling you were helping,' he repeated. 'First I thought your hand—you know, I thought your hand would come up and help—'

'It couldn't.'

'I didn't know then.'

'It was because it couldn't, don't you see?'

'No. I don't understand.'

'When I found I couldn't lift my hand, I knew I had to help another way!'

'You mean you—you prayed?'

'I never did before,' she laughed. 'Yes, it was like that—'

It was as if the windows were all thrust open into a wide silent summer, like the stillness of mountains, where there is not even the rustle of a wing. A clean perfume came in, and there was a clear seeing in Elbert's brain, as if an arc-light were burning, where only candles had shone before.

'It was so dreadful, because I had promised,' she said.

'How was that?'

'You had asked me to help you, and I had promised. Then I found I could not even lift my hand. It was then I kept saying, "I have to help him, please. I have to help him, please—"'

'I see,' said Elbert.

'And then it was as if I could see the car below—see right through into it, and I could see you and me, sort of little and broken inside, and I could feel *our* pain, but we were really together outside and above, and we knew it would be all right—'

Now he could actually help carry out her picture. 'I remember in the hospital,' he said quickly, 'when they gave me an anæsthetic, I could look down at myself like that. I wouldn't tell anybody—if I were you.'

'Oh, I wouldn't for worlds! They'd call it being out of the head!'

So she had kept all this, until he came. Just now he turned to her, and there wasn't a sound from the halls. The light was easy and flowing in the room. Everything was like a slow movement. His right foot raised to take the step toward her, but suddenly he knew if he took the step, it would be next to impossible to remember clearly that he must find Bart Leadley; quite plain, it was, that if he took this step toward her, he wouldn't be able to go down into Mexico alone and keep his mind to the allegiance he had entered with Bart's father. His foot settled back to the floor.

'... And the later part—all different—I'll never forget!' she was telling him. 'It was when the dawn came—the time we were in the awful cold—and they found us, and you were hanging forward on the wheel—your face was like stone—eyes open, but no life. Oh, I'll never forget! It was as if the skin of your face were pulled back over the bones from behind ... and they lifted me out to an ambulance, before they lifted you, and I saw your left side— all wet and stained dark ... and then I knew I wasn't helping—so frightened from your look—and I knew I must not fall into fears, nor pay any attention to your wound, but help more—from higher up, and never stop—'

It was getting harder and harder to think of the work ahead. Elbert plunged into the inevitability of it right now.

'I've got a work to do,' he said. 'I've got to go away. I'm glad I came to-day. About all this—I won't forget any of it. I'll know more about it—when I come back—'

The most astonishing thing of all, she seemed to understand even that—no resistance whatever from her, as there had been none from his father. Was it always like this—when one was sure of himself?

'I have work to do, too,' she told him at the window. 'We'll know all about everything, when the time comes.'

XVI

THOROUGHBREDS ENTER

'Cuando sali de la Habana,

Valgame Dios—'

WEEKS afterward in old Mexico. He hadn't moved straight down toward Nacimiento and San Pasquali, where Monte Vallejo was last heard of, but had followed the Border west, leaving the main highway, sinking himself into the country. He was taking it easy, learning the language from the voices in the daytime and his Spanish book at night. Days of learning— getting to know the feel of the people, learning Mamie, and that was not all—learning himself. No more leather-store; he wasn't dreaming. An old fear that something was wrong about him, even anatomically wrong, in relation to a saddle, had pretty well died out. Sometimes he even fancied that Mamie answered his rein, as if it were old man Leadley's velvety touch.

'Era la que me miraba

Diciendo adios'

That song was like an ever-continued story. A woman's voice with guitar, this time, and the old wistfulness came over Elbert—the same that he had felt in the Plaza of Los Angeles. Here he was in a little native plaza—far from travel-lines, not even sure of the name of the town, yet he had to stop and think that all he had wanted so restlessly a while back, had come to pass. At least, he was working out the old dream day by day, Sonora at her sleepiest and dustiest now, days interminably long and changelessly hot.

Though the fierce daylight had faded out the shine from her bright bay coat, Mamie was hardening to the road, and the man was coming to know some of her movements and whims, if not all. Gradually Elbert perceived also that she was aware of many of his. He never tethered her at night, yet she never strayed. He hadn't been able to learn the lip-and-finger call, the way Bob Leadley had shown him, but there was a whistle in the handle of the sheath-knife he carried, and a blast from that brought the mare in from the sweetest herbage.

He liked the nights in the open, Mamie grinding at her forage the last thing—drowsiest sound in the world to him. And her early call; out of the deepest sleep he would hear that. But by the time his eyes were open, the mare was merely to be seen feeding at a distance, her head turned away. If he dozed again, a more peremptory summons would sound, but Mamie was apparently calling to the hazy hills, her farthest concern to do with him.

One morning he didn't doze a second time, but covertly watched. About ten minutes after first call, the mare stopped feeding and came toward him, her hind feet lifting high and quickly, like a race horse, under the big blanket. Suddenly she stopped, blatted her loudest toward Elbert's partly covered head, but wheeled on the instant and was cropping again.... Fearless and winsome, a walk-trot mare, ready to go, ready to keep on, invariably increasing the pace as his hand idled at the reins, or his thoughts roamed away. Often Elbert would come to himself finding Mamie in a full ten-mile trot, when he had not been paying attention for several minutes. The pace seemed to steal upon her, and would end in a run if he did not bring her down.

One day it occurred to him that she never dropped into a walk from a trot, or back into a trot from a gallop, unless pulled up. There was no exception that he could remember. But the black night at San Pasquali had left a double-died complex at the core of Mamie's emotional self. The sound of a motor car made her unreasonable at once. She would have been glad to do the day's work over again any night, to get away from a town where machines had penetrated. Her one other deranging influence was an oil derrick. One of these attenuated triangles spoiled her whole horizon, like a finger of doom.

Gradually his rides took him farther south and west. Plenty to hear of Monte Vallejo, the bandit, of whom the peons of some districts were passionately fond. But never a word of a possible white man who rode with him. It would be a matter of luck, Elbert often thought, that would bring him up with Bart, if that ever happened. What he needed now, more than knowledge of Spanish, or anything else, and he came to know this very well, was sheer patience to carry on. It wasn't possible to ask questions about Monte Vallejo, without the people becoming suspicious at once. They thought he was somehow interested in helping the rurales, who did much of the hard work in keeping the districts in order, and yet were disliked as a matter of course by the people. Elbert often wondered what he could ever do single-handed, when the rurales for years had failed to bring in the bandit. Also General Cordano, who commanded the military of the whole country-side, was Vallejo's sworn enemy for political reasons, and yet with all his soldiers had been unable to put a stop to the activity of the bandit.

Everywhere it was related that the notorious Monte had the best horses in Sonora. Elbert was in a way to hear much of this, because the people seemed inevitably reminded of the point by his own coming to their different towns. It wasn't himself who attracted the people, however, nor held their eyes. It was Mamie whom they gathered to see, looking her over, even bringing lanterns in the evening, ever drawing near and saying to each other:

'Monte Vallejo would like that mare,' or, 'Monte Vallejo rides a horse like that.'

Many weeks passed before his task became actual. He had been as far as a hundred and fifty miles southwest, and had made a big circle north again toward the Border, when word sped from town to town that Monte Vallejo had held up a westbound Yuma Pacific train in the San Isidro Gorge, not primarily to loot the passengers—that was incidental—but to relieve two express coaches of a string of thoroughbreds en-route to the running meeting at Tia Juana.

At this very time, Elbert was in the little town of San Isidro, less than twenty miles from the scene of the hold-up.

Southwest with his new saddle-stock, the master of the road and his band were said to be galloping with three troops of rurales beating the trail behind—the latter stung and aroused as never before. Gold bar couldn't have challenged the mounted police like this theft of bang-tails.

Elbert got it all as straight as he could in his mind that night, and the next morning before full light, he filled his saddle-bags with what provisions he could procure in San Isidro and rode out, following the trail which a northern squad of rurales had taken after the bandit. He tried not to appear in too much of a hurry, but Mamie unquestionably felt the force of this fresh clue and the excitement in the air. Sonora was really wrought up. The entire body of rurales had taken the road to make a sure job of it this time. Meanwhile the people kept it a secret where the bandit's picket lines were stretched, and fixed their faces for a great laugh at the expense of the mounted police.

But the hour had evidently arrived for an astonishing turn of affairs. The second day out from San Isidro, Elbert became aware of a persistent rumor to the effect that Monte Vallejo was having trouble covering ground with his new string of horses. They were sprint-bred, but few of them took to steady distance work, so important in the present flight. On the third day, the most incredible of all announcements shocked Sonora—that Monte Vallejo and seven of his men had been captured a few miles beyond Arecibo; that they had been brought back to that town, and were being held there under a guard of rurales, as well as watched over by the little garrison of Cordano's soldiers located at that point.

No trial; only an order from General Cordano was awaited, it was said. Upon the receipt of this, Monte and his seven, without reservation, would be put to death in el cuartel at Arecibo. 'A mere formality,' the natives moaned, intimating that supplying the paper would be a pleasant task for General Cordano. This 'mere formality' sunk into Elbert's head. Later the news reached him that another wing of Monte's band had been taken. The rurales were having their turn of luck at last.

XVII

THE ART OF DYING WELL

ARECIBO was thirty-five miles away, when Elbert received this news. He did fifteen miles more that day, and the next mid-afternoon when he was close to the town where Monte Vallejo was said to be held, a most inviting level stretch of turf showed ahead. Mamie did not miss the fact. She had been well rested in San Isidro; her fitness brought to a fine point, which two full days' work had not dulled. She was teasing at the man's arm, at this very moment, and rising under him, as a small boat in open sailing after the drag of a breakwater. She took the gallop and Elbert wasn't so hard to persuade, as she stretched out, loosening her mouth from the restraint of his hand.

There was a laugh on his lips, as he let her go. These were some of their best moments together, and this particular dash promised to be a jewel among them—only in the lee of a big boulder as he flicked round a bend, stood one of the rurales at 'raise pistol,' and a snapping bark to halt from his throat.

It took nearly a hundred yards for Mamie to slow down. Elbert turning her about at length, perceived the native trooper riding his way—one of Sonora's finest—gunned, spurred, saber-sheathed on one side, carbine-booted on the other, a heavy cartridge-belt flung over left shoulder and under right arm. Around the mustacios was a restless, uncertain look.

'Magnificent horse you ride, Señor.'

'She's a good mare—just trying her out.'

'Had her long?'

'Oh, yes—' but that didn't seem to go with 'just trying her out.'

The rurale was sizable for a Mexican; not so tall, but thick in proportion; heavy wrists, bulging forearms, thick, straight back. His pony looked small and desperate compared to Mamie, but kept going with outstretched head.

'And where does the Señor travel?'

'The next town—Arecibo.'

'I also go to Arecibo.'

Mamie was now being regarded with even more than customary interest, back and forth, up and down, the rurale's eye roving, so that it was with difficulty that he kept his mind upon conversation at this time. Still Elbert was used to this sort of thing, having frequently found himself judged as a caballero of some great and elaborate house by the horse he rode.

'I have heard that the notorious Vallejo is being held in Arecibo,' he began with sociable impulse.

'Yes?' questioned the trooper in return.

Elbert wondered at the curious tone. This man had reservations.

'I have been on the road for two days and possibly am misinformed,' Elbert added carefully.

'On the road—from where, Señor?'

'From San Isidro—'

The other's hand jerked at his bridle-rein.

Now Elbert began to realize that San Isidro was hardly a town to mention—so close to the gorge of the same name where the recent hold-up had taken place.

The Mexican slowly pulled himself together to reply. 'Monte Vallejo is not being held in Arecibo. In purgatorio, at this hour, so I trust. Ah, it was magnificent!'

Mamie was now forgotten. Transformation in the rurale was to be witnessed, moreover, at this point. The man seemed higher, rising in his saddle with enthusiasm. Here was one of the pride of the Republic, indeed, having banished all present care, in the thought of the recent exploits of his troop, and especially of the light-hearted and inimitable courage of his chief, Ramon Bistula, el capitan, to whom the bandit's capture was largely due.

Tributes, dithyrambs, even—but no news.

'You say Monte Vallejo is dead—already put to death?'

'To-day. This very day, Señor.'

'And by the hand of this famous captain of your troop?'

'Si, Señor.'

'Where is your captain now?' Elbert asked at random.

'In Arecibo—have no fear. The Señor will be welcomed by el capitan Ramon, himself, who put the bullet in the head of the chief of the bandits, Monte Vallejo!'

Elbert struggled with his own composure.

'I do not understand about your captain's bullet—if Monte was already taken captive—surely he—'

'This very day!' exclaimed the rurale. 'It was so, Señor—a most charming thing! The great Vallejo had many wounds at the time—many wounds, but would not fall. Laughing, he stood unbound—his head uncovered, trying to light with wet fingers a second cigarette that would not burn —'

'I did not hear about the first. Please, not so fast,' said Elbert. 'My Spanish is of the book—not so fast, please—'

'Ah, Señor, your Spanish is quite—Castillano, quite. The Spanish of el capitan Ramon is like that, also—'

And this was the story that Elbert heard, through many repetitions, as they rode forward toward Arecibo:

'... At daybreak this very day, seven men put to death in the patio of el cuartel in Arecibo by the limping idiots of Cordano who call themselves soldiers. Seven prisoners, bound and blindfolded, shot down by the soldiers of Cordano, while Monte himself and el capitan, Ramon Bistula, laughed and smoked and chatted together, until there were no more prisoners standing, and it became time for Monte himself to stand against the wall.

'No bandage for the eyes—ah, no, not for such as he! No thongs for his hands—he waved them away; then stepping carefully to avoid the dead and shaking ones of his band, Monte took his place against the blank wall— lighting another cigarette.'

Elbert felt a frightful closeness about it all—this very day, under this very sun, the town where it happened, looming just ahead, the man at his side, having witnessed it all. Moreover Elbert was enduring a positive strain to know if one of the bodies Monte Vallejo stepped over, as he took his place at the wall, was Bart Leadley. Not without great difficulty, his pressure was so keen, did Elbert follow the details of the trooper's story, but the telling was folded over and over again on itself. It appeared that as Vallejo lighted his cigarette, taking his place against the wall, Ramon Bistula called to the soldiers not to fire for a moment, until the chief of bandits had taken one or two deep breaths of smoke.

'... Such courtesy!' exclaimed the enraptured rurale, pouring out the rest. 'And then it was, in a moment more, with a gesture of thanks to my captain, Señor Vallejo bowed his head for death, but there was not one of the soldiers who cared to put an end to such courage, and none could fire straight in any case; so "boom-boom" from the volleys and Monte Vallejo did not fall.'

Now the trooper swung his shoulders to the right and left—unsettling the gait of his pony—in the way of portraying the manner the doomed bandit kept his feet.

'Several times—in the arms and legs, struck, Señor—yet smiling still and trying to light his tobacco from which the fire had dropped—'

The trooper's speech had become very rapid; his bridle-rein changed from hand to hand, the ears of his mount cocking with the gestures. Here, manifestly, was the climax of his narrative. Once he dropped the bridle-rein entirely, needing both hands:

'... Then it was that my captain, Ramon Bistula, hastened forward, beckoning the soldiers back. He caught the reeling Vallejo in his own hands. He held him still. From his own case he drew a cigarette. He struck the match, lit it in his own lips. He placed it in the lips of the other. This I heard, "I have the honor in a moment to end the work of these frightened butchers. You are a brave man, Monte Vallejo! Speak, when you would have me fire!"

'And with that, such a beautiful look came into the eyes of the bandit chief, as he said, "Gracias, Capitan, your words and your tobacco are of one excellence!" And after that, "I will thank you now to put me to sleep, Brother Ramon—"

'It was then with his own hands—'

Florid life was closing in upon Elbert a bit too fast. Riding in silence into Arecibo, he reflected upon the quiet life of the leather-store, and upon the manner of life he was entering upon right now. He couldn't have chatted and smoked like Monte Vallejo. He couldn't have done the elegant butchery part of el capitan Ramon. It was like the story of Red Ante—there just wasn't the stuff in him to endure certain phases of that, nor the sort of thing pulled off in el cuartel, Arecibo, this very day.

In so many cases in this country, he reflected, one but arrived to the estate of manhood, when he met death in violent form. And out of all this death, what hope for Bart Leadley, and the rounding-out of that old bitter tale?

Elbert felt very confused and inadequate.

The little plaza, with only one building of more than one story surrounding, and that el cuartel, looked cold and forbidding to his eyes that late afternoon; the little shops with dirt floors, where old cheese and new rum struggled together to reproduce the flavor of by-gone Spain, had lost their accustomed romance. It was not until Mamie was safely cared for in a clean corral by herself; not, in fact, until her master sat down to tortillas and huevos rancheros (the flavor of garlic coming in from the open fireplace of the little fonda)—that a certain wistful zest of life really began to stir again in his veins once more. Black tobacco in the air, black coffee sweetened to a syrup.

'If one could only live to enjoy all this,' he reflected, leaning back.

Dusk was already in the room—candle-lights across the plaza, the first strum of guitars. At this moment a young Mexican officer appeared; elegantly dressed, and quite as Elbert might have pictured such an entrance—whipping a riding crop against his polished boot.

'May I humbly present myself, Señor—I, Ramon Bistula?'

XVIII

ONE SANG WITH GUITAR

ELBERT arose, but before he caught himself, his fascinated glance had darted to the gloved right hand that had put the closing touch to Monte Vallejo this very day. Not a bristling murderer of outlaws, Ramon appeared, but a youth of cultured turn of thought—brown eyes and boyish lips, a face whiter than his own ... uninterested apparently in soldiers, rurales, even in bandits, but asking many questions regarding America, the States and cities, the night life, and how long it took to go from Chicago to San Francisco—

'Not three days, Señor!'

'Yes,' said Elbert.

'Not three days, at fifty miles an hour, night and day?'

Like a child—or, at least, a younger brother, was this aristocrat who had taken the job of slaying out of the hands of the despised soldiers of Cordano. How many others had this small gloved hand put to death? Elbert certainly felt under a painful pull, as they chatted and complimented. Secret stiffness was still upon him, as leisurely together, they walked out of the fonda into the starlight.

'Si a tu ventana llega una paloma—' from the guitars, and by this time the girls of Arecibo were moving softly by. It was their brief hour of night, and they were abroad, eyes shining, under their mantillas; all from seven to the great age of twenty-seven, passing by the beloved captain and his friend, the American who came on the magnificent horse. What did these soft-eyed girls think of the killing manner of life of their men? Doubtless that it was all that life should be.

With his absorbing interest in America, the elegant Captain Ramon would certainly have mentioned the detail—had there been an American among the seven executed this day. Was Bart more Mexican than American? Was he regarded as a native, pure and simple, by his fellow-bandits and the rurales, or had he left Sonora altogether? These questions continually hammered through Elbert's consciousness. Meanwhile, since compliments were the order in all conversation, he was with difficulty trying to convey to Ramon Bistula how enthusiastic the trooper he had ridden with in the afternoon, had expressed himself toward his captain.

'Do all your men feel the same toward you?' he inquired.

'They are pleased with small things,' lightly said Ramon. 'To-morrow, perhaps, you will see the rest of my troop.'

'They are not all here in Arecibo then?'

'Ah, no—a third party is due to report at this time. We look for further captives with them. Six more of Vallejo's men were brought in to-day by a second squad.'

'Six more prisoners here alive in Arecibo now?'

'Yes, Señor, waiting death now in the patio of el cuartel yonder—a mere formality—the paper from General Cordano—any moment.'

Elbert turned his head away. 'Great night for guitars,' he said.

'Ah, to hear the bands of countless pieces in the great plazas of America!'

Elbert heard his own voice reach out plaintively in the hush. 'When do these further executions—?'

'To-morrow—next day—who can tell? We wait the order only. You care for these things?'

'I could hardly say that, Captain. I was only wondering at the manner in which the prisoners face the end—if an American would act the same?'

'Ah, doubtless Americans would accept with perfect composure—it is the least a man can do—'

'Are all these men calm?'

'Again, please?'

'Are they all calm?'

'Calm. I had not thought of that! They are so-so. Why not come with me now, and let us see if they are calm.'

The Captain explained that he was due to report at el cuartel at this time, but that his personal quarters were in the fonda, the picket-line of his own men being at the other side of town. El cuartel, it was to be noted, was spoken of with faint scorn, as the home of Cordano's soldiers—a poor-house and prison combined.

The two strolled across the plaza and the heavy wooden gate of the quarters swung wide. Only the front of the building had a second floor. It was like a tunnel of clay they entered, wide and high enough for a horseman to ride in, with a narrow door leading to the barracks on one side and to an office on the other. Elbert smelled the earthiness of the dried clay walls, as he passed through at the spurred heels of Ramon Bistula. The suggestions of underground began to haunt him—the presence of condemned men—this very day—the blank wall!

The passage opened to a large patio with low cells on all sides. The cells were open, the prisoners and Cordano's soldiers moving freely together. Captain Ramon informed him that for a time in the cool of the day like this the cells were unlocked, but the prisoners were returned to their quarters at nine promptly. Small fires were here and there; perhaps fifteen men in all, lounging about the fires, the guards mixed freely among them, ponies feeding in far corners. Some of the men gambled. All smoked; one sang with guitar. No sign of a face that might be an American. At least, not for Elbert's first fierce look. He noted the inner blank wall of the barracks, but dusk covered what stains might have been on the ground.

To-morrow, the next day—six more of these men to die—and they played cards to-night. Tobacco was as good to them as ever; peace was abroad ... one boyish voice sang, but Elbert remembered the underground smell of the long clay arch.

No American save himself in the prison court—no troubled thoughts save his own apparently. He moved from knot to knot among the fires, Ramon Bistula having excused himself to enter the office. The faces turned up to him from the cards, from the interminable little match boxes and papers of tobacco. The one with his guitar looked up with a gray thin smile as he hummed, but did not lose a beat of his song....

Scarred, pocked, peaceful faces—they did not seem to know any more of what was coming than the ponies in the farther shadow. There was one with the luminous welt of a knife-wound, running down the side of his throat and vanishing like the head of a worm under his collar ... boys and men.

All smoked, and one sang with guitar.

Ramon Bistula approached, but only to excuse himself again. Round and round among the little fires, Elbert moved. No, he was not as they were. It was as if in passing the clay tunnel to the little court, something had fallen from them—ghastly responsibility of self-preservation—the very thing that choked his throat now.

He had paused a second time, before the feet of the boyish figure with the guitar. The words of the song were of some curious provincial Spanish, and slowly uttered. It was this that the youth sang:

A girl once stood in a doorway and there was dust of corn upon her elbow, upon her cheek, and pale gold corn in a pile upon the mortar-stone at her side ... a girl with corn like sun-dust, shining on her skin ... with a golden bud springing like young corn in her breast.

Something like that, chaste as the light of that endless summertime. And the youth strumming the guitar seemed not to feel the great wounding of separation—but to take a vague sweetness from repeating the words—as of approach to that far doorway.

Elbert could stand the tension no longer. Through his mind flicked memories of the supper in the old barefooted woman's house in Nacimiento, of the ride afterward, of the strange, still, flowered room in Tucson. He longed to be alone, his thoughts turned yearningly toward the fonda of Arecibo; he longed to stand alone with Mamie in the clean corral behind it. A sentry, one of the soldiers of Cordano stopped him, as he started to enter the portal from the patio.

'I am leaving,' he said. 'I am with the captain of the rurales—'

Ramon Bistula now came forward from the low side door in the wall, and at the same instant, the heavy wooden gate opened from the street, and Mamie veered in under the arch, led by a soldier. Another soldier followed, bearing the big stock-saddle and blankets—Mamie entering this portal of clay! He called her name; she nickered back. Now Captain Ramon was saying:

'I trust it will not be of great inconvenience—your things being brought from the fonda for this one night—you to pass this one night here, instead of at the fonda—more air, more room—a room being prepared, in fact, for yourself quite alone.'

XIX

A CORNER OF THE WALL

A ROOM of his own. It was a cell with wooden bars, looking out upon the court where the prisoners and soldiers still played and lounged. A huge moon, almost full, came up over the opposite roof of low cells, and in the distant shadow there, Mamie squealed and let fly—a plebeian pony venturing too close, no doubt.

A sickish smile he was not aware of hung around Elbert's mouth. The floor of the cell was of stone. The wooden bars very thick, the ceiling low. There was a wide wooden bench for him to lie upon—blanket roll, saddle, and saddle-bags had been brought.... So the voluble rurale had had but one idea all the time in the afternoon; and crafty little Ramon Bistula with amiable guile—so pleasantly impersonal in leading one astray and putting men to death—Ramon, keeping him in the plaza while his men doubtless went through saddle-bags and roll. But they could have found nothing to implicate him—some silver and canned stuff. His papers of identification were in order. Then he remembered his mention of San Isidro; he would have to prove that Mamie was not one of the stolen horses. Perhaps they would think his papers were stolen, too!

The sickish smile remained—the smile of one who has seen his quest ending in failure. He thought of Mr. Leadley's affection and care for Mamie, and he had known no better than to let her show her speed on a highroad, and mention the name of San Isidro to the rurale.

His hand came up to his mouth—an ache of muscles that didn't seem to know enough to relax by themselves. The moonlight felt cold, a creeping cold on the stone floor.... The same song from the patio—guitar and corn-dust maiden—but so different, coming to him through the bars. El capitan was at the door, the sentry unlocking the cell.

'I have brought blankets of my own for you, Señor. Very soft and warm blankets. I am grieved; but it is only for the present—this interesting mare of yours—a puzzle to the soldiers of Cordano.... A very good night, Señor—'

He had actually dozed, for the plaza was empty. Elbert had heard of people going to sleep as usual, with death hanging over, but he wouldn't have believed it of himself. All was still, the moon very white upon the turf. The blank wall of the main building within forty feet from where he lay.... This very morning ... word from Cordano all that was necessary for more executions ... 'mere formality.' Now gradually, he entered one of the deep and memorable hours of his life, lying propped up against the saddle, looking out through the bars, moonlight flooding down outside, everything so still that he could hear the drops of water from the pail into the cistern in the center of the prison patio. He waited for the isolated drops, but his mind often wandered before the sound came—back to his own house in the East, to his own room, where he had dreamed so much, but nothing like this—slowly through the days at Heaslep's and the leather-store; the noon-hour in the latter place, when the door was pushed open and a certain whimsical voice started the whole works going:

'The first thing cow-people does, when they don't know what to do—'

And that very saddle was under his head! Heaslep's again, Nacimiento. His Spanish book said that word 'Nacimiento' meant Birth ... the old Señora with her castanets, and her house in the town called Birth.... Then the part he never remembered clearly, not even now—the ride to San Pasquali, the ride back; Nogales, its smell of drugs, and the Letter; Tucson and that still room where so many flowers were, still as the patio out yonder.

Until just now, he had never let himself go, in thinking about that room. Too much of a magnet about it all; it drew all the strength of mind and feeling back to it, taking the force from the work at hand here in Sonora. But this was a sort of show-down—locked up here in Arecibo. He dared now to remember that Tucson hour, moment by moment.

... And what did she mean—that she could see the car below—see right through it, and their own bodies, sort of little and broken? He knew what she meant. More than that, he knew her meaning when she said, 'And I could feel *our* pain, but we were really together outside and above.' And 'You were like one dead, yet you still drove.'... 'Your face was like stone, eyes open, but no life, the skin pulled back over the bones from behind.'... 'It was when the dawn came—the time we were in the awful cold—'

Such a stillness around her as she spoke, the stillness of the mountains. He didn't remember that dawn part after reaching Nogales, but she remembered it all. There was another thing now that he dared to ponder a moment, because he was locked up in this place of birth—no, death. 'We will know all about everything when the time comes.' How much did she mean by that?

It would likely be a lot harder to keep on looking for Bart, after letting these memories have their way, but was there to be any more mission? Was this not the end—a cell in Arecibo? His eyes focalized again on the moonlit patio. Deserted and ashen white now, but he was seeing once more the figures of the condemned men—that face of the youth with the guitar and song of the corn-dust maiden—one of the boys who had ridden with Monte Vallejo, ridden with Bart, perhaps.

Elbert had fallen asleep and awakened again to find the silvery sheen gone from the patio. Gray light was there, but no moonlight. A calling of Mexican names:

'Revas—Marcè—Trastorno—Sarpullir—'

There were one or two more, but he missed hearing the names, curiously struck by the meaning of the last 'Sarpullir'—'to be covered with flea-bites,' as he recalled from his Spanish book. Now the clanging of an iron door broke in upon him, and a thudding on the turf, which he recognized without having heard it before—the dropping of rifle-butts as the pieces were stacked. The Mexican voice was still carrying on. It made him think of the voice of the phonograph record back home, announcing the singer of 'La Paloma.'

Straight across the patio, one of the sentries was unlocking a cell door. The sentry stood back, as the prisoner emerged. Neither hurried. The prisoner made the sign of the cross, and then held forth his hand. The sentry gave him a cigarette and struck the match on his own box. Then they moved forward—out of sight.

Elbert was on his feet now, rubbing his eyes. It had all been mixed with his dream so far, but now he knew that it was really dawn and the Mexican voice was telling off the deaths of 'Sarpullir' and the others. The one across the patio had moved forward to the wall.

It was altogether incredible. The rurale's story of yesterday, all the stories of death he had ever heard, did not make the present moment believable. It could not be so, here and now.... Men fell off horses, off cliffs, out of parachutes; men were run over by cars, blown to pieces in mines, broken by many labors and inventions, but men could not be put to death—a' sangre fria—at daybreak by other men!

Now he was standing at the bars of his own cell. Something was pulling him back to the bench, but another force more rigidly held his right cheek-bone pressed between two wooden bars. Only the far corner of the wall could be seen, even so—just one man standing at the blank wall—face of a youth, looking away, head uncovered and looking away.... And now from the left, where Elbert's eye could not reach, came an old man's voice raised in wailing. It was like the voice of an old beggar at some city gate—crying out softly against what he saw, not desperately, a low mourning; and all the time the phonograph-voice gave commands—until a shock of volley-fire and a few ragged shots.

The hands of the youth lifted, as if he were treading water, as if he were pushing something from him, as if he were trying not to fall—an altogether different, divided look—the face of one being stoned, yet exalted, too—all this in the succession of shots, and Elbert had drawn back by this time, rubbing his cheek which was bruised from the wood, and there was something in him older, far older and quieter, than he had ever known before; something in him that could not laugh yet, but would sometime, something that knew that the corn-dust maiden would be waiting in that far doorway.

XX

THE TWO WHO HAD NOT HEARD

DAY was actually breaking clearer. Mamie was dancing at her tether across the patio. The recent sound of guns had not been to her liking, nor certain odors which now moved in the air. The firing squad had gathered at the cistern. The men were drinking water and lighting cigarettes, talking jerkily with laughter. The sudden surge of pity which Elbert knew was for them, not for the others.... That was his day of quiet waiting. The sun rose and steadily shone; such was a fact of continual amazement. The hours didn't drag, because his thoughts were out of himself so much of the time. He would finally feel an ache in his body and rouse from the deeps of contemplation to find that he had sat in one position for an hour or more. Queerly enough, he couldn't take his own predicament so seriously as last night.

Of course, he wouldn't give up. He would see his Sonora job through, but for the time, practically all sense of personal danger had eased away. Cordano's little infantry garrison was merely holding him until his case was straightened out. Perhaps the officer in charge had telegraphed North to verify his papers. Sooner or later he would be out of this, and if they sent him back to the States, he would return when possible and start in all over again.

Noon, afternoon. Captain Ramon appeared, commiserated with him, but announced that four more of Monte Vallejo's men were being brought in. Elbert saw the prisoners enter at nightfall, and once more, for an hour or two in the evening, the prison cells were unlocked, and after that the silence again, the lone American's last thought that there would be another death party at dawn....

He was ripped out of sleep by a full-powered neigh from Mamie. He sat up—moonlight whiter than ever upon the empty patio. Faintly he could see the mare standing in the thin shadows—that high-held listening head—the arch of her crest. He heard a horse answer from a distance, probably from the picket-line of the rurales across the town. A sentry walking past, back and forth across the entrance to the arch, paused, but resumed his pacing again.

Now, slowly, on the low roof of the cells opposite, a human figure lifted—then another. Mamie nickered; the figures flattened again. This time horses answered from both sides of the town. The sentry was slower to resume his pacing.

Elbert rubbed his eyes. The two figures on hands and knees were now moving cautiously forward on the roof of the cells toward the arch. They came to halt, as the sentry approached below. Slow seconds, Mamie dancing nervously back and forth on her tether. From one of the cells came a low grumbling at the disturbance she made—then the launching of the nearer and shorter figure from the roof, to the shoulders of the sentry, as the latter reached the turning-point of his post below.

Hardly a scream. The sentry was stretched upon the turf; the other rising from it. The second and taller stranger, meanwhile, had dropped down from the roof and vanished under the arch. Sleepy voices from the cells; a hissing command to silence; the name of Monte Vallejo spoken—another demand for silence in a tone of suppressed fury.

And now the taller of the two strangers reappeared from under the arch, leading by the hand a second sentry, who proved to have in his hands the keys of the cells. The name of Monte Vallejo seemed on every lip. Some of the prisoners in the cells appeared to know the two who had come, but kept repeating that Monte Vallejo was dead. Could it be possible that these two strangers had not heard? With this question in his brain, Elbert began to realize that the two who had come over the roof were of Vallejo's band—on a long chance to rescue their chief.

The soldier with the keys was now being forced to unlock the cells, and the way of this forcing by the tall bandit, began to fascinate Elbert in spite of his own suffocating tension. No savagery about it; the voice was cool, hasteless. Lilt and leisure in his words, as he forced the sentry from cell to cell, twirling a gun on his first finger. 'He could fan it, too—' an old sentence of Bob Leadley's flashed through Elbert's brain. The shorter bandit now hurried up, breathlessly reiterating the fact of Monte Vallejo's death.

'So I hear,' said the tall one, 'but we can turn loose the boys still alive, can't we?'

'But the soldiers are awaking, Señor—'

'I locked the door to the barracks,' coolly answered the other. 'Cordano's men will have to get down into the street from the upper windows.... We can't leave these men while we're at it. Tell everybody to be quiet. Pronto, hombre,' he added lightly to the soldier with the keys.

Sounds of the soldiers' arousing was heard from the upper floor of el cuartel facing the street.

'Pronto, hombre—' the tall bandit repeated. 'We'll fight our way to the horses—'

Elbert in the dark of the cell was folding his blankets in a distracted way, fascinated at the same time by that easy flowing voice of the tall one. He was drawing on his boots—the keys sounding nearer. Another of Mamie's nasal protests reached his ears. Would they take her? The thought actually weakened him—hardly a chance for men of Monte Vallejo to miss one of her kind in the moonlight. And now, standing at the bars of his own cell door—the tall one—that voice, the sentry beside him with the keys, wailing:

'No bantit aqui, Señor,—esta 'Mericano. Caballero 'Mericano—'

'American?' queried the bandit in English. 'Oh, I say, in there—is that right?'

Elbert cleared his voice: 'That you, Bart?'

'What the hell—?' same genial tone.

'Yes, I am American. I come from your father—'

'Open, hombre!' the command now, and, 'I don't know you. You're a lot safer where you are, but I'm letting you out.'

'I came down for you. I've got a horse—'

Banging was now heard at the lower door to the barracks.

'You'll have to saddle fast. The soldiers are sure coming-to, but they can only get out the upper windows.'

For just a second, as the cell door swung, Elbert saw the lift of a dark face—a glitter to the laugh, that low, easy flowing tone; then he was running across the moonlit patio—saddle-blankets over his left arm, saddle itself trailing from his right hand, a call on his lips for the mare to stand round. The blankets fell in place; cinches came to hand. Mamie's clean warm mouth closed over the bit, her ears wiggled straight in the head stall. Still, Elbert was the last man out of the patio, Bart standing in the street, covering the flight of his men. Shots rained down from the windows of the second floor of the barracks. A few of Cordano's soldiers had already dropped down to the street; others were crashing at the lower door which Bart had locked.

'The horses are in the hollow back of the quarters!' he yelled in Mexican.

The hand of one soldier reached up to Mamie's bridle-rein, but Bart's pistol-butt thudded upon the bone. Even in the tumult, Elbert saw that nothing escaped Bart—that he was marvelously on the job, but cool.

'Follow the others, stranger!' he called now. 'I didn't catch your name!'

'Get up here behind me, don't you want to?' Elbert answered above the din.

'Thanks, no. It's only a little ways to the horses.'

The dark laughing face was upturned again for an instant, and at this moment, from beyond the plaza across the town, came the first trumpet call of the rurales.

A rush past the small closed huts of Arecibo, women's voices uttering prayers—guttural tones of frightened men—the signal from the hollow, where other horses were waiting. Elbert saw their pricked ears in the whitish light—nine or ten horses apparently, three men in charge. The released prisoners mounted at random, but Bart cleared from the tangle on a leaping wheeling mount that looked ashen-colored in the moonlight. A cracking of rifles from behind, the soldiers now having broken out the lower door. The rurales quartered across the town, couldn't have gained the road so soon. Mamie had forged to the lead; at least, she was now abreast with the hound-bodied runner Bart sat.

'That's some horse you're sittin', Mister!' the big fellow called. 'Some more to her, too—she just can't help it, can she? And handles with a light hand!'

'Oh, yes,' said Elbert.

He felt the strangest lift in his chest—Mamie beneath, Bart and the ashen runner at his side—a sorrel, to show that color in the moonlight—scatter of shots from behind, the deep whimsical voice again from his side:

'I say, amigo mio—did you hold up a race-track special, too? They tell me I'm riding a stake-horse—old Mallet-head, here—but your mare isn't asking any odds!'

'She belonged to your father,' Elbert answered throatily.

XXI

THE RIO MORENO BRIDGE

THEY were out of the town, riding west through open country—ten men, including himself, Elbert counted, one led-horse trailing. Bart had fixed the pace of the sorrel at a full run, but still Mamie had to be held in, not to forge ahead. Finally the words from Bart:

'I don't hear much American—but that didn't sound so cheerful—"belonged," you said?'

Elbert had to stop to recall his last words. He had said the mare he rode 'belonged' to Bart's father.

'Yes, that's what I meant,' he called back. 'I came down from him—at the last—'

For a full minute, only the drum of hoofs; then from Bart, as steadily as before:

'Some night for news—Monte Vallejo and this about Dad—same night.'

'But I've got a lot to say to you from him!' Elbert answered above the roar. 'In case anything happens to separate us—I want you to know he has left you some money—quite a lot of money.'

'Struck gold at the last?'

'Yes, the mine's rich, too—a gold tooth, he calls it,' Elbert went on, absurdly. 'Only filed the top off her so far. If I don't get a chance to tell you all about it—you go to Mort Cotton, the cattleman at San Forenso—'

'Say, amigo mio, aren't you expecting to live?'

'Yes, but I've been carrying this message all summer. Been down here looking for you—long time. Remember—Mort Cotton at San Forenso—he'll fix you up, and I want to tell you, your father never forgot—but kept thinkin' about you—ever since Red Ante—'

His relief was inexpressible for a minute. He had made good, if there was not another word spoken. 'One of the finest men I ever knew!' he added.

No answer from Bart.

Now gradually Elbert began to realize he was running with what was left of Monte Vallejo's band. There hadn't been any time to think or choose back in el cuartel. He had jumped at the chance to ride out with Bart; that meant he had cast his lot with the bandits; identified once and for all with a fragment of the outlaws, now hunted from all quarters of Sonora. Still, a kind of freedom throbbed in him, his nostrils dilated to the smell of dust in the night—a man beside, a horse beneath. Finally above the thud of hoofs, Bart's voice again:

'What did they lock you up for?'

'My mare, Mamie here, I guess. They thought she was one of the race-horses—'

'Thought you were one of us,' Bart chuckled. 'How long have you been locked up?'

'Last night—or night before last—if it's getting on toward morning.'

'Two hours to daybreak yet.'

In the silence after that, Elbert became queerly aware that Bart wanted to ask more about his father, but couldn't get his voice to working. The words reached him:

'So they kicked off Monte yesterday morning?'

'Day before yesterday—'

'You weren't there then?'

'No, but they told me he had the nerve—that Bistula of the rurales, himself, finished the job. The soldiers wouldn't shoot straight!'

'I sure wanted to get to Monte in time,' Bart said, queerly. 'The game's up, with him gone—'

Did he mean he regarded their own capture as inevitable? After another pause, Bart asked: 'And what do you get, Mister, for coming down here and mixing up in this?'

'Your father arranged all that. We were friends, you know—'

'Don't you know you're in bad, ridin' with this outfit?'

'I took the job—'

'Better if I'd left you locked up in that cell. You're along with what's left of a losing game—' Bart's laugh sounded forlorn as he added: 'Why, they're after us from every town—'

Elbert cleared his throat 'You see, I took the job—'

His eye had fastened on the north star as he spoke. It was over his right shoulder, so they were riding west. He could see the mountains lying northward there in the moonlight. A sudden passion mounted in him to turn north right now; to ride straight north, crossing the Border with Bart, yonder in the mountains where there were no roads; to find himself in the States with Bart, asking the way to San Forenso; after that, the trail west to the cabin, his mind finishing the picture in a flash—with Mamie and the sorrel safe in the corral. The deep laughing voice at his left:

'I guess when you take a job, you try to see it through, don't you?'

'Yes,' said Elbert in fainter tone. He was deeply drawn to the man he had come for. Sometimes it was as if Cal Monroid were riding at his side; sometimes a feeling of Mr. Leadley's presence.

'I'd like to get you out of this, Mister, but it's a sort of tight web—'

Silence and hard riding after that; finally Bart called a halt for a few seconds to listen or get his bearings. There was a scratching of matches in the outfit as he pressed on again—the interminable little boxes and sheaves of tobacco.

'Don't hear 'em behind. The town of Alphonso is about five miles ahead, I figure. Another squad of rurales stationed there—'

'Telegraph in between?' Elbert asked.

'I'm not sure; not along this road, anyway. May be a roundabout wire. I'm taking the chance to reach the bridge of Rio Moreno. Two miles yet.'

They galloped on. The moon was tilting over toward the west. It must have been after three. He saw the lather on Mamie's neck, yet he was still holding her in. A wooden bridge loomed ahead. Bart pulled up, and turned off the main road to a parallel sandy track at the right, leading down to the water. He didn't mean to cross the bridge, Elbert perceived. The arroyo was broad and filled with stones, but the horses smelled water ahead. Mamie was whipping her head up and down, trying to take the bit. Now Elbert saw the mare's ears cock suddenly, and knew she had caught something in the wind. His hand shot down to shut off her breath, but the nicker broke out in spite of him.

An answer in kind from under the bridge. Then a volley from the same source, Elbert's second experience under rifle fire that night—venomous roaring of slugs in the air. He never could have dreamed how utterly malignant the sounds. That instant at his right hand (Bart was still at his left) it was as if the picture unfolded for his eyes alone—an upturned face, then a crumpled, falling body, horse leaping aside—empty saddle—one of the four released from the prison at Arecibo. In the midst of the shots, a yell from Bart:

'We split right here, men!'

Elbert heard certain names shouted—those who were to turn back, those to ride north. Then Bart's face jerked around to him. 'This way for us, Mister, we ride together.'

Their horses were at full run, along the river-bed, where the clear sand showed at the edge of the stream—shots still peppering after.

'Your mare!' Bart laughed. 'Why, they'd have gotten all of us, if she hadn't given warning! We'd have gone right into their gun-barrels under the bridge!'

'She's one more listening mare,' Elbert called back.

XXII

FRAMED IN A DOBE GATEWAY

NORTH, they were riding straight north, though the going for a way was a bit heavy through the sand and stones.

'Not so fast quite!' Bart warned. 'The other three can't keep up—'

Elbert was bending forward because the rurales were following, their shots still in the air. His heart was filled with elation that Mamie had given the warning, and that their course had turned north. He had forgotten the three of Bart's men still riding with them. More shots from behind, a queer gulping cough from Bart.

'Are you hurt?' Elbert called.

'Yes, one of 'em got me. I've—been—hit—before—but not so close in—'

Elbert's hand tightened; his eyes still held to the north star. 'Can you ride a ways?'

'Sure. Long as you do—'

'Don't forget to give me a warning, if you're going to—'

'I'm not going to fall, amigo mio! They'll never get us now, but our three behind—we're ridin' too fast for their ponies!'

Elbert did not look back; nor did he check Mamie's speed. This was the instant he realized he was in command of affairs, if anybody was. His momentary concern wasn't with the three bandits, whipping their ponies to hold the pace, but with the one who called him "amigo mio" and bent forward now as if pushing the saddle from him.

The sorrel galloped at Mamie's side with great easy leaps. To keep going with Bart was Elbert's game, not with this remnant of Vallejo's band; to keep going north with Bart at any price; to turn loose the horses faster and faster, their heads to the north—if only Bart could stay in his seat! The river road running north assumed clearer outline—wheel-tracks, a hardening pebbled way. Again from his companion:

'We're ridin' too fast for the others, Mister—'

'I think we'd better not wait for anybody now, Bart. This is a running match right now, while you're in the saddle. Who's got the stuff—that's what we're going to find out—Mamie here or your Mallet-head!'

A chuckle in answer. 'You're the doctor!'

Elbert bent forward. 'I say, Mamie, we're off!' She knew that tone—a wide-open throttle, it meant, and the big sorrel settled lower at the left, his fish eye fixed on her nose.

Now part of Elbert's private reaction to the headlong pace was the sense that he had been fixing for this race all his life—a sort of climax of all days, and his eyes glanced often up to old Polaris, as if the north star were a silver cup for the winner. A distance-course, seconds pounding on into minutes, the minutes into tens, dusk of earliest morning blent with the low moon's rays; only two horses in the finish, silence as deep from behind now as from the desolate foothills ahead—a friend to stick by at his left—white smile, two slits of black for eyes, body hanging forward.

Every little while: 'Don't fall, Bart! Give me a word if you're slipping!'

'I'm not going to fall, Mister—'

The river had narrowed to a creek; the road to a path; the blowing horses pelted forward on rising ground—

Then it was all as queer as a dream. Breaking day, a face framed in a dobe gateway, a face by the side of the road. Just a glimpse—girl or child or woman, he did not know—but a face in the ashen light—oval beauty in the gateway of a dobe wall! Elbert's head flung back as they passed, but the face was gone. That instant thickly from Bart:

'Pull up, pardner!'

Elbert's hand went out to the left, as he drew Mamie sharply in with the other. The look of death was on Bart's face; his lips moved.

'Big town ahead—Fonseca—three miles or so. Rurales—they'll be waitin' for us there—' The gamy head rocked back, the spine drooping sideways.

'We're not going there,' said Elbert, leaping down. 'God, how you've sat it out! You can fall now—I'm underneath!'

'I'm not goin' to fall—' Bart mumbled, but his hand relaxed on the pommel.

Elbert looked forward and back; not a sign of life either way, but the face at the dobe gate was strangely before his inner eyes. Something queerly to do with the song of the corn-dust maiden in that far doorway, it seemed to have for him. His face lifted to the cold gray of the dawn-lit sky. Rurales still following possibly ... 'mere formality' ... blank wall ... oval beauty.

Now he was carrying Bart back, leading both horses.

'I'm taking a chance to get you a berth,' he gasped, coming in sight of the dobe gateway, now empty.

An aperture in a dobe wall for a gate—face gone. Over the gate as he led the horses into the yard, his eye caught the letters formed of faded tile, 'El Relicario.' He fancied the movement of a dress through a low arbor ahead. Still with his burden, he moved toward it.

She was there—in the doorway of a broad low dobe ruin. He seemed at first to see only her wide eyes. And then his Spanish came to him and words inspired by another's need—pressure he had never felt back of an effort before.

'Look, Señorita—he must have shelter and care—my companion! Will you not give help to him? I will pay a great price!'

The girl made no sound, her eyes fixed on Bart's back, where Elbert's hands pressed a dark saturation.

'May I take him into your house for shelter, Señorita?' he panted.

She led the way indoors, halting in a large, all but empty room.

'There are those who want his life,' Elbert said unsteadily under his burden. 'May I not take him farther in?'

She turned instantly toward an inner door.

XXIII

FENCELESS FOOTHILLS OF SONORA

THERE was a room in which he saw a full-sized harp in its shroud; there was a trellised patio, two great ollas standing on the heaved tiles and jasmine vines very thick and ancient. At the far corner, in the gray morning light, stood an elderly man with bared head. To him, the señorita gave the signal of silence with her finger touching her lips, and also to an old woman in the latticed kitchen.... Ruin of an old plantation house, very large, some of the windows unglazed; El Relicario—the name ran through Elbert's brain which throbbed from the stress of his burden—all this a matter of seconds only.

Then a corridor and a little room to the left—queer warmth rising in Elbert's heart, as he placed Bart upon a cot that had recently been slept in. The sense came to him that this was a kind of sanctuary—a cross upon the wall, a white flower beneath, the girl standing against the wall, her arms slightly lifted, her hands toward the long booted figure on her own cot. Elbert bent over Bart now—a rush of memories of the day he had brought his father to the cabin and set him down like this. The eyes were looking up to him; the lips moved with hardly audible words.

'Back at the gate—as we turned in—the tracks of our horses!'

'Yes, sure, I'll fix them.' Then he added: 'Listen, can you hear me, Bart?'

'Yes, sure—'

'I'm going to ride on and leave you here. I'm taking both horses—so the rurales won't stop, but follow me on. I'll hide in the foothills to-day, and circle back here to-night or to-morrow night.'

'I hate to see you go, but you're—you're the doctor!' Bart laughed. 'About the sorrel—he knows the whip, but goes mad under a spur—just a pointer in handling him—but you know a horse.'

Elbert's jaw hardened. 'Thanks, I'll remember,' he said.

The voice went on faintly: 'I didn't miss how you handled the mare!'

'You didn't miss—anything!' Elbert replied, fearing the other was delirious from his wound.

'Sorry—you go—'

'It's the only way. Adios, Bart—and to you, Señorita, this—'

He placed two gold pieces on the table, but saw her hurt and troubled look, as she came forward from the wall.

'You see, I'm leading them away from him!' he said, as if the point were of great moment to her.

Bart's hand lifted; but his face was cut off by the girl's bending profile. Queer joy lived in him from Bart's recent words about his handling of the mare, but a sudden weariness came over him, too, as he turned away. A nicker outside answered his step as he hastened across the broken stonework of the patio. Mamie had never before been left unceremoniously to cool in a yard—in company with a stranger.

He led the horses out to the road; no sight or sound so far at least, from the direction he had come. Leaving them standing on the highway, he reëntered the gate and began fanning out the hoof-marks in the yard, using his broad hat. Out through the gate again, he worked until all was clear; then mounted and pushed on, leading the sorrel.

Day was brightening among the foothills. The big range he had ridden toward through the night was now intimately uncovered on his right hand; Fonseca, three miles straight ahead, Bart had said. Both horses were pulling toward the creek. They were too hot for a deep drink, but might have a few draughts without harm. Besides, he must replenish his pack-canteen.

The sorrel fought to drink his fill. Elbert had to climb into Bart's saddle to get the big fellow out of the stream. Back on the road again, he followed for about a quarter of a mile, toward Fonseca, before turning eastward to the mountains. He had left a clear trail so far, and now off the road, he began to weave back and forth along the stony waste, following a vague idea to confuse and delay pursuit, being well past the old dobe house. Bart would have done all this better, he thought, recalling how the other, half dead, had not forgotten to tell him to wipe out the tracks leading from the road in through the dobe wall.

Many minutes afterward, he came to a halt upon an eminence and looked down, at a frail low smoke pattern of the town to the north. Also he glanced back to familiarize himself with the lay of the land around El Relicario. The hills shut him off from much of the road; he caught no glimpse of possible pursuit. Still later in full sunlight he halted in a rift between the hills and forked out a few mouthfuls of breakfast from a glass jar of frijoles, packed in his saddle-bags at San Isidro three days before.

Now in a rush it closed upon him—the heaviness, the coldness, the blur of fatigue. Languidly, he set to work upon the horses. They were sweated out, cakes of dust and salt at the cinchlines and blanket-edges, both restlessly athirst, but apparently not lastingly hurt by the long gallop of the night. He took off only one saddle at a time; holding the other ready instantly to mount and be off at the first sight or sound, working meanwhile with wisps of grass and cloths from his kit. Strange, it seemed, to play the groom to another than Mamie; unfamiliar, the bones and textures of this rangy gelding; no curiosity or particular affection from the sorrel runner such as Elbert was accustomed to. Running was what this one knew, but Mallet-head was presently adapting his taste, nevertheless, to the scant sun-dried grass with better grace than the mare. She couldn't see why a stop should be made in this waterless, fenceless wilderness. Standing by, she nudged the man's arm repeatedly for light on the subject.

'Night-running's all right with her,' he mused, 'but she doesn't get the inconveniences of being a bandit's mare.'

His thoughts were running queerly from so many shocks and tensions. The sun was well above the eastern mountains, but not yet nine in the morning—just about the time he used to be getting to the leather-store. Fenceless foothills of Sonora, a wearing grind of thoughts and questions. Little inner room—cross and white flower and cot so recently slept in. Did the señorita always get up so early? Were the old people her parents? How had it all been arranged with so few words, as if some power intervened to help in a pinch? Was Bart going to live, or would it be as it was with his father? Had the rurales by this time stopped at that open dobe gateway? Had it been yellow of him to run away from the other three bandits?

He began to think he had done rather poorly. If Bart had held the lead, he wouldn't have run away from his men. Bart had spoken of the matter three or four times after his wound, and then given up—'You're the doctor!' In the thick bruised feeling of his brain, Elbert's depression deepened. He recalled his bad judgment in letting Mamie out—so close to Arecibo, and in telling the rurale that he had come from San Isidro.

The sickish smile came again to his lips. He wasn't much for this sort of life; he ought to be driving a car, a truck, possibly. He recalled his funk in the prison at Arecibo, even before he was locked up, and afterward in the cell—and how the bandits had given themselves to death. '... peaceful to be with like cattle. I don't mean they're cattle, only that they loll around and ruminate like 'em,' old Bob Leadley had said, summing up the whole matter in the remark that he wished he had treated the Mexicans as well as they treated him.

Moreover, the old man had found out that there were times when a man couldn't wash his hands. 'Wasn't that just what I did about the other three?' Elbert questioned, squinting up at the sky. Now a painful rush of pictures went through his brain—the wall in the prison patio, the corner of the wall—only yesterday morning—standing at the bars of the cell.

He caught himself rubbing his right cheek.

No, there was something in him that didn't belong to this sort of life. As for Red Ante, he couldn't have done the thing Bart did—he couldn't have lived through it, as Bart's father did.

All day the horses kept their heads turned down hill. They snipped the sparse grass—eyes and ears and muzzles stretched toward distant hollows—all instincts fixed upon unseen water. Elbert didn't trust the sorrel, not even to tether him, but kept a hand on his bridle-rein. Once he dozed and was awakened from a thirst dream by the sound of horses sucking in water from a stony stream.

... Mexico with her quaint, gentle ways—a plaintive singing voice 'carved out of starlight'—but underneath—violence. Men fell to killing each other. Just so much of all this killing a man could stand, and no more. How had Bart stood it for so long? Bart wasn't like that, himself. He hadn't even roughed it with the soldier of the keys in the Arecibo prison—not even in that moment of fierce danger and haste! ... and that easy flowing voice of coolness and laughter and daring, but how had Bart dared to put Palto out of his misery?

Elbert pondered a long time, finally remembering how he had felt the need of carrying Bart deeper and deeper into the house, as if he had known all the time there was an inner room. When he reached there and had laid his burden down—a sudden sense of peace had come over him. What was the meaning of that? With his eyelids closed he saw a light shining through alabaster. Yes, he had met one who would know the meaning and could answer this.... But what was the meaning of the power that had seemed to come to him to make the señorita understand with so few words?...

Cross and white flower—Spanish-faced girl standing back against the wall... Elbert dozed again, and the inner room of El Relicario and the still flowered room of Tucson softly, magically folded into one. It seemed quite easy and natural.

A grim day, his nerve at lowest ebb, nothing of the lift or glow he had known in moments of last night's riding with Bart. Would they ever ride together again? Was Bart lying dead now in that inner room?

Fenceless foothills of Sonora—ages in a day! He didn't feel quite sane, riding down to the creek in the dusk at last. He couldn't hold his mind to thought of danger, but to water only. Mamie smelled it and could scarcely be held in; the sorrel plunged at her side.

XXIV

SHEATH-KNIFE

IN full darkness he left the two horses fastened among the alders of the stream bed and started for the dobe house. At least, there were no horses of rurales waiting at the gateway of El Relicario, nor any lights to be seen in front; but moving around to the side, he fancied a faint ashen shaft farther on from an unglazed window. He knocked. A pall seemed to have fallen upon the world—before the step, the moving candle—and the señorita's face, finger pressed across her lips as she pointed to the little room. Then he was following her candle through the passage.

There was Bart—bloodless, startlingly altered, but asleep, not dead, as he had thought in the first flash. And presently, Elbert began to feel himself standing about like a stranger. Either he hadn't seen straight at daybreak, or the señorita had become a woman since then; no face of a peon girl by a lonely roadway, this woman of El Relicario to whom he had offered coins, but of one risen to emergencies, as only quality and breeding can arise. She had led him out into a hallway and was speaking as one who had found her place and work in life.

'He will be so glad to hear you have come. I have said you would return, but he could not be sure. There is food for you waiting—please come.'

He followed her through a firelit room, where the elderly man he had seen in the patio in the morning, arose and bowed with courtly grace, and from behind him the faded-faced woman smiled in the manner of far-off times. A wooden table, a pitcher of milk, corn-bread and rubbery cheese of goat's milk—but Elbert hardly tasted what he put in his mouth.

Horsemen had ridden by in the early morning to Fonseca, the señorita told him, an unusual thing, but they had not stopped, and others had passed later, going the opposite way.

She left the room and returned, dragging a small sack of grain for the horses, which Bart had asked her to procure, and there was a package of food for Elbert's need of to-morrow—all this spoken of with frequent gestures toward the wounded man in the little room; her every thought and sentence apparently blent with something Bart had said or wished. Yes, he would live, she repeated, but his recovery would take many days. Then Elbert heard his own words in careful Spanish of the book:

'Tell him I shall be waiting—that I will come again to-morrow night or the next night—that I shall wait for him until he is ready to travel—'

'You mean to leave now—at once?'

'Yes, I see that he is being well taken care of. The horses might call to any horses traveling by—'

His words were getting slower and quieter, but there was in his body and brain an intolerable burden having to do with the thought of to-morrow—not only to-morrow, but 'many days.' It had been all he could do to live through to-day. Now he left her, knowing she would steal back to the little room at once. He crossed the inner garden, the room of the harp, nodding to the elders, crossed the yard, passed out through the dobe gate—in unbroken darkness, moving toward the alders of the creek-bed.

His feet dragged; the early night, so dark that he had to keep constant thought to the road, burdened by the sack of grain over his shoulder. Still distant from the alders, he began to listen for Mamie's signal, but the sound of trotting hoofs came instead.

One horse only, coming his way, no accompaniment of wheels. He let down the grain-bag at the side of the road, instinctively aware that if either of his horses had pulled loose a hunch like this on his shoulder would make any effort at capture practically impossible in the dark.

'Hoo-ooo, baby, easy, little one!' he softly intoned. He could see no movement yet; the hoofs were still. Then like an explosion, a snorting blast of fright from the horse ahead—not Mamie. He well knew her protest of fear. 'Come in, kid—easy, old-timer!' from his lips, as he moved forward very slowly, his fingers closing at last upon the broken bridle-rein of the sorrel.

The big runner was standing almost rigidly in the dark, as Elbert made a quick tie of the two shortened leather ends, his ears still straining for a sound from the mare. He mounted, but had difficulty in turning back toward the alders. The gelding fought the bit, tossing his head. The man's unspurred heel knocked his ribs, but the runner snorted like a crazed colt at this, standing straight up, and Bart's warning about the spur flashed back. Elbert, getting control again, snatched off a small branch as he brushed the foliage at the road-side, and the sorrel started forward at a stiff-legged, unwilling trot, still unruly as he neared the alders.

The mare was gone. Holding to the shortened bridle-rein, Elbert was on his knees, lighting matches—an ashen smile on his lips. Yes, he actually smiled at himself now—so miserably hopeless a few minutes before, just at the thought of waiting days. Something to be dismal about now.

Countless horse-tracks among the alders, conveying nothing to his eyes. Passing rurales had possibly heard the horses, and tried to take them. Possibly one of the police had mounted the sorrel and attempted to force him with a spur. That might account for old Mallet-head breaking loose.

Elbert rode slowly on toward Fonseca, head bowed. Yes, they had given him something to be dismal about all right. What hope—if they had taken her into town.

He couldn't brace into Fonseca and attack the town single-handed. Still he kept on, until—it was almost a sob that surged up in his throat—the sound of a nicker—far to the right! His hand darted forward to the muzzle of the sorrel to shut off possible answer. No need of that. The big gelding was unconcerned about that far-off sound.

Mamie—letting him know! He could tell that call of hers in the midst of a herd of horses; and the rurales or whoever had her, were not pushing on to Fonseca, but eastward toward the mountains. 'I'm coming!' he muttered. He flicked his branch on the sorrel's flanks.

Minutes afterward, the call again; and presently from over the eastern mountains, appeared the moon, a shaving less full than last night.

Last night—that moon from the cell of Arecibo—far-off as childhood.

Two hours, at least, of fierce strain—following those whom he supposed were looking for him; finally a faint haze of firelight over the rim of a hill just ahead—the mysterious party having come to a halt. If they were rurales, why hadn't they gone to Fonseca—why this halt in the open? He was close as he dared to be with the sorrel. Even now, the big stake-horse might undertake to announce his presence and need of forage. Elbert turned him back to a live-oak scrub, made him fast, and retraced his way up the slope again, struggling with weariness and many fears. The moon was now well clear of the eastern ridges.

On top, he gradually discerned two figures stretched out in the firelight below—in ordinary Mexican garb, not in uniform of rurales. Moving nearer, he presently made out Mamie, still saddled, a third Mexican sitting on the ground at her head. Seconds crawled by, as he waited breathlessly, with a vague hope that this third one might doze, but nothing of the kind. Instead, the Mexican now rose, leading his charge to a low tree clump, where other horses were faintly to be discerned.

Evidently the Mexican was about to fasten the mare. Once tied, there was less chance for her to break clear, than from the Mexican's hand. Only a second or two to think in; in fact, Elbert didn't think it out. His fingers reached for the handle of the sheath-knife, bringing the whistle to his lips.

Its shrill scream cut forth. Mamie's head lifted and yanked back, but the Mexican did not lose his grip upon the rein. Running forward Elbert whistled again; then stretched his lungs in a yell, as strange and startling to himself as to the sleepy Sonora hills.

The knife in his hand was not to kill; he had merely not put it back in its sheath. The two men by the fire were on their feet; the third stubbornly trying to gain the saddle, but Mamie slid from under, and kept pulling away. Then an instant of utter amazement—the face of Mamie's tormentor near enough to be recognized—one of Bart's bandits whom he had raced away from the night before.

Elbert changed the quality of his shouting, but the Mexican had let go the bridle-rein, and was speeding after his two companions, who had vanished from the circle of firelight. They were at their horses—mounting and spurring away. Elbert rubbed his dazed eyes—they were gone—Mamie trotting toward him, head extra high to keep from tripping on her bridle-reins.

The whistle had done it—and his shouts, which must have sounded like a platoon closing in, to the leaderless bandit party. The whistle for Mamie, the yell—Elbert did not know how he had come to vent that, unless for his own courage.

Never before had he felt such a sense of belonging anywhere, as when he folded over the Pitcairn stock-saddle. Sitting straight did not suffice; he seemed fallen to clinging to the neck of his mare. Even a minute later, he would have forgotten Bart's sorrel, tied securely in the bristling live-oak scrub, had not Mamie flirted her signal as she galloped by on the moon-drenched hill.

'They sure thought I was the rurales,' he laughed.

At this juncture he missed his saddle-bags.

'I suppose Bart would go back and get them right now,' he thought. 'Not for me. Nothing in them I can't do without. What silver there is—those three fellows I ditched last night—may need that!'

His eyes were craning about the sky to locate the north star.

'I won't have to tell Bart how I lost Mamie, nor about the other three,' he communed later. 'Now that I've got her back, I won't have to speak of it at all.'

It was a different matter about that grain-sack, however. The horses would need that, and another drink from the creek to-night, before facing to-morrow in the brown and sultry hills. He made the big circle to the Fonseca road and the alders, but was back in a star-rimmed mountain wilderness two hours before daybreak, the big gelding taking an occasional nip at the grain-bag as he trotted along.

XXV

ELBERT LEARNS TO WAIT

NEXT day Elbert climbed the foothills and explored the mountains eastward. He found many tracks of water, stream-beds of the rainy season, but it was now autumn, the dryest time of the year, and hours passed before he followed a trickle up a dim ravine to its first pool. He had to grant that it was the horses that helped him locate the water in the first place, but there was queer satisfaction about the experience, as if he had been marooned on an island and his life depended. No water ever tasted just like that. He watched the horses drink and graze, and made them stand for a half hour at a time in the sludgy grass at the side of the stream, while he stared up from the shadowed cañon to where the sunlight burned on the ridges. 'Only one thing better than water for a horse's hoofs,' old Bob Leadley had said, 'and that's more water.'

No further need to cross the Fonseca road night and morning to reach the creek. He would risk a night-call at El Relicario once in a while—grub for himself and forage for the horses, but the old ruin was now fifteen, possibly eighteen miles, and Bart was in good hands.... One by one, Elbert beat back the days, though he actually lost count, even before it became apparent that Bart Leadley was going to live. During his first two or three calls at the ranch house, there was a good deal of doubt on this main point. From the very beginning, the big fellow weakly pressed him not to stay.

'No use of you hangin' up all these days in the mountains, Doc,' he said. 'I'll follow north across the Border, as soon as I can make a break.'

'But I'm getting to like it out there,' Elbert would tell him. 'Only lonesome a little at first. Why, there's no place I could leave the sorrel for you, if I went. The rurales would know that horse anywhere.'

'Take him along. I'll get a cayuse, somewhere—'

'No, Bart, I came down here for you. That's what your father wanted—for me to bring you back—'

The other's eyes held the low ceiling. 'I'd hate to have you *after* me,' he laughed. 'I mean like a sheriff—'

Elbert conned this all next day in his high solitude. He couldn't get it quite clear. Surely, no sheriff would ever suffer from hopeless spells of faint-heartedness such as he was given to.... They were oddly embarrassed with each other in those first talks, but when silence became oppressive, Bart would enquire regarding some detail concerning the horses. On this one subject alone, Elbert expatiated.

'A little grain from here is keeping them fit,' he would report in effect. 'And say, your Mallet-head sure has an appetite,' he once observed. 'Mountains agree with him. He flavors up his forage with all sorts of new leaves—even pine needles. Mamie's more particular.'

Elbert caught a gleam from the cot. Bart's black eyes were holding him. 'You like 'em, don't you?'

'What?'

'Horses.'

'Sure,' said Elbert.

'I knew—the minute you climbed on that mare in front of the quarters in Arecibo. We were a bit in a hurry right then, but you didn't jerk her round. I got to know pretty well before daylight that you were a real hand with a horse, Mister.'

So Bart was really fooled. He had said something of this kind before, that first daybreak here in El Relicario, but Elbert had feared then that his mind was wandering. He didn't answer now.

'I like these people,' Bart was saying, about the Mexicans. 'I get along with 'em pretty well, but they don't savvy the horse. It doesn't seem to run in the blood. Monte Vallejo who had all Sonora thinking he was a caballero— even to Monte, a horse was something to ride to death. All these people saw and hack and ride on the bit. That's what got us into trouble with those race-horses, and that's what got to me from you, the first minute in front of el cuartel—to see a white man sitting a horse and knowing what he was doing and what her mouth was made of.'

'Your father told me all about Mamie,' Elbert said.

'All the telling in the world wouldn't do it, if a man didn't have the feel of a bridle-rein on his own hook.'

It was like being called to the carpet to be presented with a diploma or a medal—no time for Elbert to trust his voice to relate that Mamie was practically his first experience, and that only a few months ago.

'How was it that the race-horses got you into trouble?' he asked.

'We couldn't manage 'em. They were used to being babied for the track— used to the sprint; didn't know anything about saving themselves for distance-running. There was a lot of young stuff among them, and all our old cayuses were done for. We tried hammering the bang-tails to the road, and they went crazy.... I drew the prize of the lot. All old Mallet-head knows is to eat and run—so long as you keep the spur off him!'

'He keeps his feelings to himself, so they can't be hurt. He's sure rugged,' said Elbert.

Sometimes Bart seemed to be listening for a step as they talked; and when the señorita appeared in the doorway, Bart's eyes and hers would meet and cling for a second.

There began to be a secret heaviness connected with this for Elbert. What would happen to her when Bart left the little room of the cross and the white flower?... So much taller she seemed, than in that first moment in the dobe gateway. Had he seen her then as now, he might not have asked her help. Perhaps, even if he had not heard the song of the corn-dust maiden, he could never have thought of imposing as he did that morning upon Valencia Vidaña, the daughter of El Relicario, now a dobe ruin of many rooms, but in its day one of the famous ranch-houses of Sonora.

'Great name in these parts in the old days,' Bart once whispered. 'Valencia's father was one of the big men of Sonora under Diaz, but everything's broken down since. Loot and confiscation's the trick here—worst of all from Juan Cordano. We happened in the right house. The old don told me the other morning, he had hoped to see Monte Vallejo in Cordano's place here in Sonora.'

Long talks concerning all that led to Elbert's coming to Sonora. Bart's deep laugh once sounded in the little room.

'I'm used to Mexicans,' he said. 'I don't know much about the States. I s'pose there are a lot of people up there you can trust offhand, like Dad trusted you.'

'You see, he had to have somebody interested in Sonora, and willing to do a lot of riding,' Elbert answered. 'You know, he wanted you to have Mamie, but he wasn't sure how long it would take me to find you—a chance even, that I might not. He didn't want her to change hands another time. He always thought about her feelings—'

Elbert found himself staring at the little crucifix as he talked. Bart didn't seem to be troubled as much as he was—about the feelings of the one in this house.... One night after about ten days in El Relicario, Bart turned over and drew his right shoulder clear from its covering to show how the wound was healing.

Elbert cleared his throat. 'I don't see how you stayed in the saddle from that bridge until daybreak when we got here,' he said hoarsely. 'Why, that bullet would have knocked me out of the saddle like—like—'

He had quite forgotten—'clear through to Nogales.'

A low laugh again. 'Say, amigo mio—say, Mister, you're sure nervous as a filly, about being caught makin' a move like a gamester!'

Elbert conned that all the next day in the hills.

XXVI

SILENCE

MEANWHILE he was learning undreamed-of-matters about himself. No amount of riding such as he had done down in the valleys could have shown him what he was getting now, in the stillness and sunlight and starlight of high country. A hundred times a day, the flick of a lizard over leaf or pebble or twig called his eye; that was the only continual distraction. The days were mainly silent, though the nights were full of sound; the coyotes sometimes a maddening chorus that stirred up unheard-of deeps in the listener, and once as he lay awake at night a muffle-winged owl swept past so close as to fan his face. That shook him like the sounds during his first night out in White Stone Flats. In the stillness, thoughts rose up in him with a power he hadn't known before; one could get so accustomed to this sort of life, he reflected, that he would be entirely unfit in a little while for the towns again.

Here's where a man reverted to type. What he was at bottom came out. One might sink into being just an animal—eating and drinking and sleeping—or get more fiery alive with the days, more quick and sensitive with strange inner activity. There were times when Elbert's thoughts carried him along with a clear cool strength that was almost frightening. He knew now that he had never been alone before; that a man isn't quite alone, even if locked in his own room—that he is only really alone with the sky above and the earth beneath.

He had told Bart that he was getting to like it, but that didn't become wholly true until quite a number of days had passed. Again and again he felt his jaw hardening, his lips pressed together; gradually his fears fell away and the silence bit into the very center of his being. He became a part of the outer silence of the days, a part of the fierce still sunlight that slowly blackened his hands and face. He looked back upon his dreams in the room at home, remembering the things he had treasured there—Indian blankets, pictures, leather work—all had meant something.

Out of these kid treasures and symbols, Cal and Slim had come to life, Heaslep's, Nacimiento, San Pasquali; Bob Leadley, Bismo on the Rio Brava, Red Ante, the Dry Cache mine; Sonora, the cells, the corner of the wall, flight from the rurales, El Relicario. He could shut his eyes and think way back to the very beginning—hear the swish of motor cars from his bedroom window, the sound of the piano below, the sounds of his phonograph, and that last swung him swiftly across the continent to the Plaza at Los Angeles—'Cuando salí—' and the leather-store.

All these a part of him now, but in the beginning there had only been a little room of books and pictures and yearnings—yearnings that finally drove him out to find his Crimson Foam. Something else he had found—that still room in Tucson. Not a symbol of that in his father's house—oh, yes, of course, the alabaster bowl in the dining-room!

His thin lips stretched into the beginnings of a smile. He had heard it said that each day brings to a man nine parts review and one part advance work. Everything seemed like review to him now—the whole circle rounded (at least, it would be when Bart and he were safely over the Border into the States) everything review, except that still room in Tucson. Very much advance work, that. His heart pumped so that he could actually hear its beat.

Sometimes he felt, if he could get a little deeper into the silence, he would know all about—even that. Anyway, it began to dawn on him that everything would have been spoiled if he had rushed north alone, leaving Bart—that the greatest adventure of all lay right in the core of these days of solitude and silence. One night he felt like a different man altogether, as he started down toward El Relicario in the dusk.

XXVII

WORDS

'YOU see, I was lazy—no two ways about it—lazy, from the very beginning,' Bart said during one of the night-talks. 'I can see how Dad felt now. I didn't know any better than to think he was against me in those days. I got the feeling I was wronged, and that's bad. It's bad to let that wronged feeling pile up in a kid's chest, until there is no seeing it any other way. The thing that hurt me most was about that horse—old Rat-tail from the Cup Q.'

Elbert kept still with effort. He knew the story of the rat-tail from Bob Leadley's telling, almost as well as Bart did, but the latter got to talking too rarely to be interrupted.

'A bad name, that horse had, but he wasn't really bad. A horse isn't like a man; he isn't like a dog. A horse is more like a woman—he goes by feeling, not by his head. A dog will dope a thing out; a mule will, but a horse feels his way. Why, that mare of yours—I'll bet she doesn't miss much that's goin' on, even if her back's turned. You're not foolin' her a lot, even if you think you are. She's cute as a woman—

'The more a man knows about a horse, the more he respects him, the more careful he is,' Bart went on. 'You never see a real hand yank his horse around or flourish none. You're apt not to know a real ridin' gent unless you're one yourself. He works easy, and doesn't attract the eye. You never see him starting a horse into a run as soon as he leaves the corral—unless there's mighty pressin' business, like that night we first got together. You don't see him rowel or quirt, because a real hand doesn't bring up a horse to need stimulants that way. And he isn't botherin' with one that does—not for long. Nine times out of ten a bad horse is man-spoiled, and a real hand doesn't care to mix with other men's botched jobs.'

Elbert couldn't help but see Cal Monroid in all this—Cal, and the way he handled and sat old Chester. Bart and Cal were curiously alike in the one utterly cool and nerveless quality. Evidently it was in this quality, first of all, that their mastery over horses lay—no nerves to confuse the feelings of a mount.

'That old gray had been raked and hooked so long that all he knew was to fight back. Everybody over at the rancho was afraid of him. Of course, the fellows didn't say they were; they're more afraid of each other finding out that they're afraid, than they are of what they're afraid of—'

'I can see that,' said Elbert.

A curious look came into Bart's eyes—a trace of deep rest. 'You see, a horse knows when a man's afraid. He smells fear, or feels it. He gets afraid, too, or confused—loses what little head he's got. He begins to look out through a sheet of blood, if you drive him deeper into fear. If pushed far, he goes crazy, and that's what they call a bad horse. Sometimes they are ten times as strong as a horse in his right senses—just like a man-maniac—'

Elbert had so much to say it was hard to keep still.

'You see, I wanted that old gray so badly for my own,' Bart went on. 'They told me how bad he was, but I couldn't believe it. He let me get up to him—let me climb on his back. But when I got him back to Bismo, everybody remembered him bein' an outlaw. Dad tried breakin' him again—and they took him back to the Cup Q.'

Bart chuckled. One would think he had been telling some amusing boyhood experience. His voice was easy, almost careless—Bob Leadley all over again—not a sign for the listener that a deep misery of life was being discussed. Suddenly Elbert realized that it was not only with horses, but with men like Bob Leadley and his son—one had to trust his feelings, or else miss a lot. And with women—

'But your father knew better afterward,' Elbert finally said.

'How's that?'

'He knew you had something on the rat-tail, he didn't have—'

'How's that?'

'He told me. Everybody in Bismo kept warning him that the gray would kill you. He got afraid *for you*, but he knew better afterward. Your father came to understand what you meant about not wanting a 'broke' horse. He told me he thought about that one thing for years. It was from him and some things from Mort Cotton—that I got any idea about handling Mamie—' Deep relief, Elbert knew as he halted a moment, the same that he had known that night, as they rode away from el cuartel in Arecibo. He was making it all clear at last. He got a queer feeling, as if Bob Leadley were resting easier, too.

'One of the squarest men anywhere, your father,' he went on. 'He knew you had something on Rat-tail that he didn't. He knew that "breaking" a horse is old stuff. He said he had belonged to the old school that thinks a horse is ruined if it ever gets its own way. One of the things he liked to say

- 119 -

best was that there are a whole lot of good riders, but only once in a long while a good horseman—'

'But he didn't understand about Palto.'

'Oh, yes, Bart. Even Mort Cotton did.'

'They didn't think I did right, did they?'

'Yes,' said Elbert.

'Foolin', aren't you, amigo mio?'

'Not on your life! He and Mort Cotton were crazy-tired, all shot to pieces—that night in Red Ante. Of course, Letchie Welton only had his idea of law. Why, your father thought it out for years, never got over it—his part—or rather, what he didn't do. Kept saying at the last that a man can't "wash his hands."'

'Took it hard?'

'Rather, but he understood it all at the last. Mort Cotton did, too. It was Mort who said at the hearing back in Bismo—that the most merciful shot he ever heard fired was yours that night before you rode out of Red Ante.'

'I'm sorry Dad took it so hard.... You see—you see, I couldn't get Palto loose. He might have lived for days—until they got him to a place where they could string him up—'

The next day alone in the mountains, Elbert found that the old story of Red Ante was slipping out from him—that it didn't hurt any more, that it would be difficult, and likely unnecessary, ever to talk about it again.

XXVIII

'LIKE THE VIRGIN SPEAKING—'

FINALLY came the night when Bart said he would be ready to ride within a week, but just then they heard a light step in the next room, and Elbert's voice became very hushed.

'I've been looking for a way north through the mountains. My idea is to take it easy, riding nights—keeping our eyes on—'

'On what?' Bart asked.

'On the north star,' in embarrassed tone.

'Why, we're not thirty miles from the Border right now. We can do it in a night.'

'But I've been thinking we'd better not enter Arizona on any of the regular roads—and there's quite a ride west after that—'

Señorita Valencia was in the doorway.

'You're the doctor!' Bart laughed.

Two nights later Elbert made Mamie fast in an old lane about three hundred yards from the Fonseca road directly back of El Relicario. This was his next to last trip from the mountains down, according to the plan. He was to bring both horses next time, two or three nights later. Then north and west with Bart through the high range, which he had explored so many days with the one single thought of ending his mission.

Nearing the old ranch house, he moved around in front to approach by the road, but heard Mexican voices before reaching the gateway. Stealing closer he saw three ponies standing just within—carbine-boots and saber-sheathes! Only the rurales carried that outfit. He moved back and circled among the scented vine-tangles of the grounds, at length drawing near an unglazed window of an empty room, which was just across a corridor from the little room where Bart lay. Faint reflection of the candle-light came from there, careless strumming of a guitar and laughter of the Mexicans from the front of the house.

A light step at his left, a movement of white, visible as he turned— Valencia, alone in the grounds. Softly he called her name.

'Oh, I prayed you would come, Señor! The rurales are here. They have seen him! I have left them but a moment—saying I must dress—' She was all in white, her face held close to his, the breath of her whispering part of the perfume of the dark.

'You must take him away to-night—now, while they wait—or he will have to go with them! You see, they are not quite sure yet, it is he, but have sent for others in Fonseca who will know. Before the others come, while I keep the ones here in the front of the house—you must take him to the mountains—to your country!'

'Have they got Bart in front with them?'

'No, he's still lying in there—but one of the men is watching in the corridor. I have told them how ill he is!'

Elbert spoke swiftly: 'I'll go and bring the mare closer in, Señorita, and be back to this window in ten minutes. Get word to Bart that I'm coming back!'

'I will try—or perhaps my mother. They are waiting for me in there now. I must keep them in the front!'

He heard the Mexican voices. 'In ten minutes—' he hastily whispered.

He was running back toward Mamie's tether. No moon, but a few great stars, fireflies in a near low tree—a perfumed, humid night. Thoughts ran with him. It was like the mystery of life—her pale upheld face in the dark, with an untellable meaning for his heart, having to do with a corn-dust maiden. Even as he ran, he marveled that she could help him get Bart away 'to the mountains, to your country!' ... the breath of her whispering—

Mamie was dancing, as his hands ran over the cinches. 'The job of our lives!' he panted. 'You're fit, little one. Won't be your fault if we don't make it! It's for him—for old Bob Leadley, Mamie!'

He was riding back. He could not bring the mare too near to the ranch house, lest she signal to the rurales' horses standing in front. He reached the unglazed window of the unused room. Perhaps she had been unable to get Bart word, for he had not come. Perhaps, the full ten minutes had not passed.

He waited a moment, then climbed into the empty room, crossing softly toward the faint sheen of light in the corridor. Reaching the door, he could look across the corridor into the little room where a single candle burned. Only the foot of Bart's cot was visible.

Now a step sounded down the corridor at his left. He drew back into the dark. A Mexican approached, glanced into the little room, then turned back toward the patio—the rurale pacing his post.

Elbert craned forward as far as he dared; this time he saw the covering of the cot flung back, a single booted leg beneath. Something familiar in the way it jerked that second, made him know that Bart was drawing a boot on the other leg. How could he let Bart know he had come? The slightest whisper was as impossible as it was for him to cross the corridor while the sentry moved back and forth.

At this instant a liquid shower of chords sounded through the house—the great harp in the front room coming to life—Valencia's voice lifting above her accompaniment:

'Cuando sali de la Habana,

Valgame Dios!'

A heart-break in itself—that song.

At the same time, another voice from the patio—quavery tones of the old señora offering the sentry a glass of wine. Was she trying to hold him at the far end of his post? Now in the opposite doorway, tipping a little weakly, hatless, without coat, but fully booted, Bart Leadley showed himself, a cool laugh on the dark face. Elbert darting a glance down the corridor, saw the back of the rurale's head. He thrust out his hand to steady Bart across the corridor.

'... Era la que me miraba

Diciendo adios—'

They had crossed the empty room; Elbert outside the window, was helping Bart through—the rurale still held to the patio-end of the corridor by the señora—or was it by the song? Even in the fierce drum of his excitement, words of old Bob Leadley flashed to Elbert's mind: '... like the Virgin speaking to them.' Yes, he could understand being held by that song; a wonder above everything, that Bart could leave at all.

'Qui es mir persona

Cuentale tus amores—'

They had crossed the grounds to Mamie's tether; Bart's left ankle was in his hand for a lift. He swung up behind on the spacious saddle-tree; Mamie darting off in the dark toward high country with her double burden. Hauntingly from behind:

'Me la han matado

Me la han matado—'

And from Bart:

'That there song, Mister, has followed me all the way!'

Miles back among the hills, they picked up the sorrel; still no sound of pursuit. Then it was northward among the foothills—the north star for Elbert's eyes. At any moment he half expected to hear, 'No, I'm not going to fall, Mister,' but to-night it was: 'Don't worry about me. I'm sittin' easy.'

Before daybreak they followed a little stream up higher—less volume but more noise all the way, and came to rest in the deep privacy of a sunless ravine.

The second night, long after midnight, they heard the far scream of a train from the north.

'The Mexican Pacific,' suggested Elbert.

'Where?' said Bart.

'That train—'

'The Mexican Pacific cuts north through San Isidro Gorge ten miles southeast of here. Ask old Mallet-head, that's where we dragged him out of his Pullman—'

'You think we've crossed the Border—that this is a U.S. Transcontinental?'

'The States is a large place, but I sure thought you'd know home when you got there, Doc.'

But Elbert could hardly believe. A little later they caught a glimpse of the crawling serpent of coaches, faint lights for scales. Finally in the first daylight the two horses crossed the tracks—'Safety First,' authoritative like an Eleventh Commandment on a big water tank in the dusk of morning.

XXIX

HIGH COUNTRY

THEY found the highway north of the railroad and turned their horses west.

Bart looked a bit white and shaky but made no sign to stop.

'Don't you think we'd better lay up for a day or two in one of these towns, so you can rest, Bart?' Elbert asked.

'I'm not sleepy,' said the other. 'I'm gettin' what I need outdoors, and aboard old Mallet-head. I always did need the outside of a horse to pull myself together.'

As it began to get hot in the morning, they veered into the hills and found shade, resting several hours.

'How far west of Nogales do you think we are right now?' Elbert asked.

'About a hundred miles, I'd say. You see Fonseca lay a long ways west of the main road south from Nogales, and we've kept pushin' west through the mountains since then. We can find out by askin' along the railroad—'

'I'm figurin' we might not have to go to San Forenso first to get to the cabin,' Elbert said. 'You see, San Forenso is still farther west from here than your father's mine—'

All through the recent weeks in Mexico, Elbert had felt his mission would end when he safely crossed the Border with Bart, but now he knew a secret restless urge actually to reach the cabin, before letting even Mort Cotton know.

'You see, everything we need is there,' he added.

'Lead the way, Doc.'

The second morning afterward, Elbert looked up into a range of hills, remarking that he thought the Dry Cache was up there. 'San Forenso is twenty miles ahead, and we'd have to circle back, if we went there. The mine must be straight up from here. Yes, I think those are our mountains, all right,' he added. 'I remember your father said you could look over into California and back into Sonora from just above the mine—'

'It's giddap with me. Persuade yourself—'

But the mountains that had looked so feasible from the railroad turned sinister and rebellious as they climbed. Forty miles around would have been simple to the twenty they had made before sundown that day—a waterless fight all the way. They were in the big timber of the altitudes again in the lengthening shadows, and Elbert looked at the man beside him, riding on hard gray nerve; then at the drooping head of his own mare in front. He had given in to a sort of mania to get into high country. It had been getting clearer for hours that he should have gone straight to San Forenso, from where he could have been sure of his way to the claim. It might be best to turn back to the railroad now—while there was a bit of light.... Just at this instant Mamie's ears pricked; her body came to life under the saddle. The sullen eye of the gelding caught a flash of her new fire.

She broke into a trot, starting down-grade. They crossed a sloping bench of big timber and checked down into a valley open to the western light.

'I don't see any trail, but she's sure got an idea!' Elbert called.

'She sure has,' Bart panted, 'and I'm for it—'

In the open, she veered swiftly to the left, making for a cañon mouth, and then in letters writhing a little before Elbert's dazed eyes: 'Are You Doomed?' on its white rock! The living fact of the Flats broke upon him.

'Why, we're home, Bart!' he gasped. 'The cabin's back a ways. She's makin' for the last water—'

'First water I've seen in some time,' came from the other, as Elbert helped him down.

There was dusk and wood-smoke; the grinding of the coffee-mill, the sputter of bacon oil for flapjacks, a deadlock on the matter of whether a can of Michigan pears should be opened or Hawaiian pineapple—finally both, for it was a fiesta night at the Dry Cache mine, and the stores were endless. They had fared slim for some days and ridden hard. Few words, because Elbert felt a bulge in his throat from the pressure of unfamiliar joys. After supper, he left Bart and led the two horses, in their 'cooling' blankets, down to the last water to finish their deep drink for the night, also to refill canteens. Bart came out of the cabin, as he returned, and they sat down in the clean straw when grain was fed, leaning their backs against the fence.

That astonishing sense of unity crept over Elbert that he had known once or twice before. He remembered Bob Leadley's story of when he was a little chap, leaving the supper table where there was a fight on between his father and mother, and going out into the barnyard where the cattle ruminated, and there was peace. Yes, he must have listened deeply to all Bob Leadley's words. It was almost as if he had been that little boy; almost as familiar to him as that night of tequila in Cienaga, in his own experience, when he had sat with Cal and Slim (Chester and the Indian and Mamie grinding at their sun-parched corn). A warm breeze fanned his face now with a smell of sunlit rocks and pine bark and that carried him back to the night of that warm wind at Heaslep's ranch, when Cal and Slim asked him to join them in a ride south, where he was going anyway. Exquisite ease in the very fatigue that closed in, delight of relaxation complete for the first time in his life.

The next day they didn't stir far from the claim, only moving about the different patches of sun and shade to stretch out in the deep languor that followed days of strain.

'Pretty near everything a man could want here—don't you think?' said Bart.

'Pretty near,' said Elbert.

'The old man made it all to suit himself, didn't he?' the voice drawled on. 'Always a great hand for keeping things up, Dad was. Left his mark on everything. I can see it now. A kid wouldn't—'

'I think he was making it for you all the time,' Elbert said, 'just as if he was writing a letter to you, when he built those cabinets and stored them. I know he was—always thinking you would come back like this.'

'A lot of work in that tunnel for one man to do alone,' said Bart. 'Must have taken him a year—'

'More,' said Elbert.

The next morning at breakfast a curious quiet settled between the two men. The spell was breaking, a different gleam in the eyes of the big fellow across the table. In a wordless fashion, Elbert sat for a time. Another sentence of old Bob Leadley's cleared with deep meaning. 'I'd get lonesome for him when he was right in the same room—'

'We'd better not wait any longer before letting Mort Cotton know,' Elbert finally said. 'I'll ride down to the Slim Stake and get him on the telephone—'

He was back within four hours and Mort reached the claim before sundown. It took two days for everything to be settled, and Elbert was tired in an altogether different way at the end. He had done more talking in those two days than in all the weeks in Sonora.

'Bart,' he said, when they were finally alone once more, 'there's nothing I'd like better than to work that gold tooth with you, but I'll have to be away for a few weeks.'

'Which way you headin', Doc?'

'East. Been away from home for a long time. I've got to see my father—' Elbert caught that strange gleam again in the eyes of the other. 'And my sisters,' he added.

'I'm ridin', too, Mister. For a while—'

'You're not going—you're not going back?'

'Back into Mexico?' the other laughed.

'I thought, perhaps—'

'Why, you don't seem to believe I like it here,' Bart chuckled. 'Pretty near everything a man could want—'

Just words, perhaps, Elbert thought. He didn't see how Bart could forget. He couldn't have, if he had been in Bart's place.

'Oh, yes, I like to look and listen around here,' the big fellow went on, 'and back in that tunnel there's a message for you and me all right, but no hurry, as you say. We'll wait a little longer for that. A whole lot of times down in Sonora I've wondered just how it would feel to turn loose in an American town—Tucson, for instance.'

'I'll be stopping off in Tucson,' Elbert allowed.

That day they rode down to San Forenso and left the horses at Mort Cotton's ranch. Elbert planned to take the night train.

'I'll stay on with Mort for a day or so,' Bart said. 'I might hunt you up in Tucson, if I get there before you leave. They say there's a hotel there—'

'The Santa Clara,' said Elbert.

He looked back toward Mort's corral, as the old cattleman was bringing the rig to take him to the station. He moved to the gate and let himself in. Mamie walked toward him, but halted with lifted head, in the afternoon light, as he had seen her the first day, only now her coat was faded by many sweats and suns. Her head lifted higher. She was listening for something no one else could possibly hear—

'One more listening mare,' Elbert whispered.

Her forehead presently bumped his shoulder. Farther off the sorrel stake-horse was sniffing at the cracks in Mort's hay-shed.

'I'll be coming back, Mamie. Oh, yes, I'll be coming back—'

XXX

TUCSON AGAIN

IT wasn't a dappled gray this time, but one of the same breed. Elbert was abroad in the streets of Tucson, long before the city was astir, his train having set him down at an unseemly hour. He passed a harness shop and peered in through the window, where his eye encountered the cocked ears and pointed head of a wooden horse. Evidently its place was the sidewalk, daytimes, being wheeled into the shop at closing-hour on castors.

It was as if he were in the Plaza at Los Angeles again. It was more: like a man coming back to find his old nursery unchanged. Elbert's lips moved.

'Wouldn't Mamie shy if she passed that palfrey on a lonely road?'

His hand pained. He was clutching the arm of a rocking-chair. He had left a network of invisible foot-tracks over two sections, at least, of the city of Tucson. The day was now advanced to eight-thirty in the morning, and he was back in his room at the Santa Clara. His strong, blackened fingers relaxed on the oak. He arose and pulled down both outer windows. He went to the hall-door to feel that it was locked. He took off coat and vest, wiped the sweat from his forehead, called a number at the telephone.

'May I speak with Miss Gertling?'

'Miss Gertling—why, she doesn't live here any more—'

'Does she—where?'

'She's only here part of the day—some days—'

'Could you give me her address?'

'Who is it, please?'

'Mr. Sartwell—'

'Oh.'

'Elbert Sartwell—'

'Oh,—you're—wait a moment, please!... Yes, Mr. Sartwell, you may call—' the snappy tone had softened.

Elbert's mind fumbled the number, but he got it down.... His second call was entered. A man's tone advised him respectfully not to disconnect. Then out of the smothering stillness:

'Hello?'

'Mary Gertling!'

'Yes.... Oh, I know ... and where are you?'

'At the Santa Clara.'

'Will you come over?'

'Yes.'

'Oh, wait! I know better. I'll come for *you*! In the street in front of the hotel—in ten—fifteen minutes.'

He bathed a third time. He was below watching the street both ways. Crowds were passing, by this time—on the way to work. Elbert's feelings were torturingly divided. Sometimes he pitied all these people going to work; sometimes he envied their calm matter-of-fact seizure of life. As for himself, he seemed dangling in space, having lost his clutch entirely.

The crowd jostled him back against the entrance. It must be a half hour. Could there have been a mistake? His eye verified the fact that it was the Santa Clara hotel he was standing against. Many faces coming from the right, as many more from the left. He would hold his eyes one way, until he felt she must be standing at his back. Yet it was from neither right nor left that her call came—from the throng of cars in the street, a roadster pressing in toward the curb. She was alone. She had opened the door. Like that day in the flowered room, he had been listening and watching toward the hall and she had come from the porch.

'I gave you a ring at the Finishing School,' he said, as if he had been waiting months to say just that.

'I finished last June, but stayed on part-time for other work there.'

'Post-graduate work?'

'I've been learning to ride a horse. I thought you might come there first.'

Any one could see she had driven a car for a long time—queer ease of her own, no thought. She straightened her dress and thrust her wrap back from her shoulders, as if ready for all day. The small boot poured gas with mathematical accuracy and steadiness.

They were out of heavy traffic now; passing through an end of town increasingly familiar to Elbert.

'Everything has seemed tangled and lonesome during this last week,' she was saying. 'But before that, it all grew clearer and clearer.'

'How do you mean?'

'For three weeks, just before this last, everything seemed to get clearer and clearer.'

'Why, those were the weeks I spent in the mountains,' he said. 'I was alone all the time, and high up. It sure was a change coming down, though. Last few days, it seemed my mind was trying to make up something that never really happened. Hardest of all, just before I got you on the 'phone this morning.'

Yes, it was the Border Highway they were on. She was at his left. Gradually he was breathing better. At first he had thought she would have to hurry back, but that thought was slipping away. She wasn't speeding, but pressed the car forward steadily, as if making a day's passage. It was a white dress she had on, a sort of linen—like a handkerchief. The white road stretched ahead, very straight, but gently rolling. The sense of on and on came to him. He had always felt like fighting when with a girl before—except in that flowered room—but there wasn't a fight in the world to-day. The wide empty road stretched ahead for miles; a film of dull shining vapor gleamed over the top of each rise, but always as they rolled up to it, the film vanished, showing up presently above the next. They never arrived, always approaching, as to a mirage.

'Sometime we'll get to know it down here on the roads and even in the midst of the city,' she said.

'You mean that sense of clearness—I spoke of having in the mountains—?'

'Yes, we must not lose it anywhere—as we did last week. Why, I thought some of the time you weren't coming back—'

'I thought some of the time, you weren't expecting me to come back,' he said with a shiver.

They were running through Harrisburg of trucking days. Evidently she had no mind to return—Heaslep's beyond. It would break in upon their day to stop, yet she had chosen the way. He couldn't tell her to go back. He had wanted to see Cal and Slim, but not to-day. Still, she kept on, the ranch-houses finally showing ahead.

'I know 'em there—we'll have to call, since we're going by. That's where Cal and Slim are. At least—'

'Shall I turn in?' she asked strangely.

'Yes.'

He saw the faces jerking out from the farrier's and the cook-house, one or two Chinese. Elbert nodded and gestured, but not an eye turned to him, all cooling upon the one at his side.

'Drive on to that door marked "Office,"' he whispered.

Frost-face appeared in the doorway. Elbert's fixed smile of greeting had not yet registered for a return glance. Frost-face began lifting off his wide hat. Elbert couldn't remember ever having seen before that hard white head, uncovered.

'She's some—car,' Frost-face said suddenly.

'We were just ridin' by. Thought I'd—' Elbert began, but the foreman wasn't paying attention. Finally in the strain Elbert pursued:

'Any sick cattle?'

'No, but we're on the watch. Is she a six?'

'No, an eight—straight eight. Thought we'd like to see Cal and Slim—'

'Up in Wyoming—when I heard last—playin' the round-ups and the rodeos.'

'We were just ridin' by,' Elbert said.

'I hear Slim sat Poison-face for twenty-five seconds at Cheyenne.'

'Are they coming back?'

'Ain't likely. They—you see, we're using tourin' cars mostly to ride range and keep up fences.'

Now Elbert received his first direct glance. 'I see you're wearin' everything but your likker this morning,' Frost-face remarked.

'I'm starting East,' said Elbert.

'Round by Panama?'

Elbert chuckled. 'I mean, I'm startin' East to-morrow night.'

'Takin'—the filly?'

'No, she's back in San Forenso. You'll sure remember me to the boys, won't you?'

The roadster was rolling quietly out of the ranch driveway. Mary turned the car south toward the Border. No word about it.

Twilight—Nogales—they were having supper in a little Yaqui restaurant There were paper-thin leaves of corn-bread baked in the sun. He was looking away toward the South.

'Sometime we must go clear down to the señora's house in Nacimiento where we first met,' he said.

'I don't know. We can't ever find what we're looking for by going *back* to any place. It's always ahead.'

'What we're looking for,' he repeated, but not as a question.

'It would seem so easy to find; it would seem so easy to keep,' she went on, 'but I don't know any one who has kept it. Certainly none of my girl friends who have married. I don't even know what it is exactly.'

'It's something that's kept on building. Really started when I was in the hospital—no, before that—at the explosion.'

'No, before that,' she said.

'Did it?'

'Yes, at the barefooted woman's, where you were so firm. And then something really happened to us in that ride back from San Pasquali, when we were not in our heads.'

'I had your letter in the hospital.'

'And then, that day you came to the Finishing School.'

'That was a great room to me,' he said.

'Every day has been different, but it has kept right on building.'

'Especially in the mountains.'

'Yes, wonderfully then—until last week when I spoiled everything, by getting so nervous and expectant.'

'It's been building all day to-day—with me,' said Elbert.

'Yes,' she helped, 'differently from ever before. And to-morrow night you are starting East—'

'It will keep right on, won't it?'

'It must, but it's so easy to spoil—that's what frightens me. You wouldn't think it could, only you see so many others who do—who have.'

'It couldn't be with us.'

'I think everybody says that at first. You won't let me spoil it, will you?'

'I was going to ask you that.'

'But you are so firm. You must always be like that. Why, it's all because you were so firm that first night.'

The day was passing fast as a theater scene, but in the last moments of Nogales, he kept thinking of the seventy miles back to Tucson. At least, they had that much left to-day.

'Won't you drive back?' she said at last.

'Not unless you're tired?'

'Oh, no, I don't think about it.'

'Then you—'

Sixty miles still to go. She was driving slightly under 'thirty,' but the minutes were racing by. She didn't go any slower. Fifty miles. The roadster kept its pace, the meter staying around twenty-eight or twenty-nine, always between twenty-five and thirty. Forty miles; then half way. She didn't cheat.... Stars, sage, warm wind, early evening.... A thoroughbred, always different.... What could possibly be spoiled, if two kept on and on like this? But she knew something; and others, he knew, certainly had spoiled it.... Twenty-five miles.

The night suddenly opened for him. He was nearer to her than ever before, though he had not changed position. He could not feel himself or her, but there was a white ball of light between his eyes—like all the stars of the gray haze fusing into one, like all the perfumes of the air fusing into one, all the stillnesses he had ever known fusing into one.

'You—' from her.

'Yes, I'm here—'

'You know something—I must know!'

'*You are something—I must be,*' he went on, as if finishing a magic formula which she had begun.

'Oh, what has happened to us?' she cried suddenly.

'I don't know.'

'Do you suppose—the others—ever know anything like that—like this?'

'I don't know,' said Elbert.

'If they did—I don't see how they could ever go apart.'

Lights of Tucson, streets. The amazement that he knew now, was that she had kept on steadily driving.... '*You are something—I must be—*' Had she said that, or had he? Had it really been spoken at all? And the car hadn't halted a moment.

'But we must never stop—no matter how wonderful it is—and say "This is it,"' she repeated. 'We must always keep on and on—'

'It's so very much—right now—'

'I know—I know it is—but don't ever let me stop and say: "We've found it."'

The car drew up at the curb of the Santa Clara.

'To-morrow. Luncheon. I'll come at twelve—right here.'

Then he stood upon the pavement, differently alone.

It was after 11.30, next morning. Elbert had sent a telegram to his father that he was starting East to-night. Passing the desk he saw a paper in his box.

'Friends of yours in Suite 14,' it read. No signature. Writing he hadn't seen before.

He stood still for a moment. It wouldn't be necessary to go up right now. She would be in front in fifteen or twenty minutes. He might let the message wait until afternoon. But after that, perhaps they would be going out somewhere. Better now, yet the hush he was in was hard to break. It was like a spell, yet the elevator door stood open.

It wasn't Bart who opened the door of the upper room but the old don of El Relicario, and graciously behind him, biding her time, the señora. Then from an inner room (was the crucifix there, too, and the white flower?) came the corn-dust maiden.

'Ah, Señor, you were so brave—it was all because you were so brave!'

And behind her sounded the easy flowing laugh—words from Bart:

'Everybody here but the rurales!'

'Only—' said Elbert, 'only my friend—a girl—I'll get her now—and bring her up.'

THE END

Milton Keynes UK
Ingram Content Group UK Ltd.
UKHW011057250424
441751UK00004B/213